PIPPA AND FRIENDS
INVESTIGATE
THE MYSTERY OF THE MISSING TEAPOT

MARY MOLONEY

CANDY JAR BOOKS · CARDIFF
2024

Published by
Candy Jar Books, Mackintosh House
136 Newport Road, Cardiff, CF24 1DJ
www.candyjarbooks.co.uk

ISBN: 978-1-917022-00-2

Editor: Shaun Russell
Editorial: Keren Williams

Printed and bound in the UK by
Severn, Bristol Road, Gloucester, GL2 5EU

*To my beloved John for always playing
Sherlock Holmes to my Watson.*

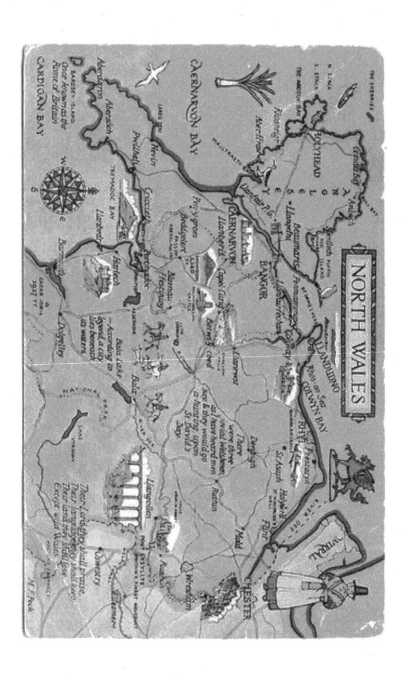

NORTH WALES

Chapter One

In Mabel's Branches

Everyone was sitting around the breakfast table drinking tea when the cuckoo sounded.

'That'll be Richard, I expect,' said Grandpa.

'How lovely,' said Emma. She rushed to open the door, red curls a-flying. 'Do come in, Farmer Richard.'

'Yes,' said Granny, smiling her sweet smile. 'And, please, have some tea.'

'How are you all? And how are you getting along with the trumpet, Ed?' Richard asked, rumpling Edward's fair hair.

'Amazing,' said Edward, Emma's little brother. His large blue eyes widened. 'I'm sure I'll be in the brass band soon.'

'Glad to hear it,' said Richard. 'I would've brought you some eggs, but I haven't got any. Either the hens have stopped laying or someone's been stealing them. It's a real mystery.'

1

Emma's ears pricked up. 'How long have you not had any eggs for?'

'About two weeks, I guess. But I lock the henhouse at night so I really don't know what's going on.'

'It's very distressing to think someone around here may be a thief,' said Granny.

'People are not always good,' said Grandpa sadly. 'Well, Richard, to cheer us up, why don't you sing for us?'

'Oh yes, please do,' chimed the others.

'I will, if you insist,' said Richard modestly. He stood up and launched into song. He had a fantastic tenor voice which was why he was Emma's hero. None of them could understand why he wasn't performing on one of Europe's opera stages. He also looked the part with his dark hair and eyes, and rosy, smiling face. When he had finished, they applauded wildly and Pippa the poodle pirouetted on the spot in appreciation.

'Goodness,' said Richard in surprise. 'A mouse has just popped out of Ed's pocket!'

'Ah, that's Louis Armstrong,' said Grandpa.

'Edward,' scalded Granny, 'how many times have I told you not to put Louis Armstrong in your pocket? You could squash him.'

'Oh, Granny,' began Edward. 'Louis Armstrong's much too clever to be squashed and he hates being left in his cage. He came out to listen to Richard's singing.'

2

'Well, a farmer's work is never done so I must get back to it,' said Richard with a smile. 'I just popped in to say "hello".'

They went out into the garden, Granny taking her half-finished painting and brushes with her, and waved Richard off.

Emma smiled as she saw the tall, broad figure of her grandfather going into the garage to tinker with one of his machines, which was his favourite pastime. His still startlingly blue eyes lit up if he managed to get them running – and he sometimes did, with the aid of string and rubber bands. So, the garage contained a motley assortment of appliances such as mangles, clocks and old engines, which seemed always to have been there and probably always would be. One of Grandpa's recent adaptations had been to replace the doorbell with a cuckoo's call.

Emma walked across the grass to the greenhouse to pick one of the tomatoes growing there. As storms and time had destroyed much of the glass in the greenhouse, it had been replaced by old raincoats, sweaters and scarves, with a jaunty trilby perched high up at a rakish angle. Nevertheless, the tomatoes were the best she had ever tasted.

She went around the back of the house, near where the broken-down old caravan was parked, to find her grandmother with paintbrush in hand, critically surveying her picture of daffodils. Granny always managed to look elegant despite her old clothes, because she was very slender with beautiful silver hair and green eyes, just like Emma's.

'What do you think, Emma dear?' she said.

'It's lovely, Granny – you are clever.'

Granny smiled her sweet smile and said, 'It is quite good, isn't it? Is Gramps still playing with his machines?' and they laughed.

By this time, Grandpa had also appeared. 'Where do you think Edward could have got to?' he said.

At that moment, the door of the caravan flew open and Edward, dressed in a duffle coat and a huge felt hat, attempted to blow a fanfare on his trumpet.

'Edward, dear, that's enough for the time being. Really, Ernest,' she said, in a stage whisper, 'why ever did you have to buy that trumpet?'

'Oh, Edith, it's not often you find a good quality trumpet in a junk shop that's small enough for a child to play, and learning to play a musical instrument is one of the greatest gifts in this world.'

'Well,' said Edward, pushing his hat off his face in order to speak, 'I'm much better at it than I was last week!'

They laughed and Pippa barked in agreement.

Looking at her watch, Emma realised that it was almost 11.30am so she and Pippa walked quickly down the lane, waving to St Mary Magdalene church as they passed. Then they ran across the field to an

4

apple tree called Mabel. She and her friends, Lizzy, Laurie and Katie, tried to meet up in Mabel's branches as often as possible and they had made a vow that they would always meet at eleven thity on Saturday mornings, come what may! Some time ago, Lizzy had observed that the apple tree looked as friendly and welcoming as her Great-Aunt Mabel in her green apron, so 'Mabel' had stuck from then on.

Emma was the first to arrive so she greeted Mabel, putting her arm around her trunk. At that moment, she saw Lizzy, a tall slim figure, with long, straight, light brown hair, walking across the field. She was dressed, as usual, in her favourite colour, purple. They waved and smiled at each other. By then, delicate, blue-eyed little Katie was crossing the field towards them.

'Where's Laurie?' said Katie. Just then, they saw an out-of-breath Laurie racing to join them, her thick, dark hair soaking wet.

'Sorry I'm late and that my hair's so wet!' exclaimed Laurie. 'I've just been swimming.' Laurie was an excellent swimmer and currently working towards her Brownies' Advanced Swimmer's badge.

'You're always late, Laurie,' said Lizzy teasingly. 'Even when you haven't been swimming!' And they all laughed.

The girls had chosen the sturdiest of Mabel's branches in which to sit. Lizzy, as the most agile, climbed up to one of Mabel's top branches, with the others sitting lower down. Pippa lay at the foot of the tree, grinning up at the girls from time to time.

'Guess what?' Emma paused. 'You know Richard, the singing farmer, who lives next door to us? He told us just now that he hasn't had any eggs for two weeks, and he hasn't a clue why! It occurred to me that, with the Easter holidays starting soon, we could try to solve the mystery and it would be great to help Richard.'

'I do believe you have a crush on that man,' said Lizzy roguishly.

'Not at all,' said Emma, blushing and looking offended. 'Just because I admire the man's singing doesn't mean that I would ever indulge in such nonsense.'

'Now, girls, let's not quarrel,' said Katie sensibly.

'You mean we could be detectives?' asked Laurie, her dark eyes lighting up. 'How thrilling.'

'But what shall we do exactly?' asked Katie.

'It seems to me that we need to catch the culprit red-handed,' said Lizzy. Her grey eyes looked thoughtful. 'The thief must come at night or else he'd have been seen.'

'Why don't we go to Richard's farm one night and watch to see what happens?' asked Emma.

'Do you think it'll be dangerous?' Katie looked apprehensive.

'Where's your spirit of adventure?' cried Laurie.

'Since there are four of us, I think we should be safe enough and Pippa will protect us, whatever happens,' said Emma. 'Let's meet under the oak tree at the entrance to Richard's farm at ten o'clock next Friday night.'

'That's all very well,' said Katie, 'but how am I supposed to get out of the house without my mum noticing?'

'I guess we'll have to pretend to go to bed and then sneak out quietly. I don't know about you, but my mum and dad seem to forget all about me when I've gone to bed,' said Lizzy.

'Yes, it'll be great fun,' declared Laurie.

'Well, I'll certainly do my best,' said Katie weakly.

'So, all in favour, say "agreed",' declared Emma.

'Agreed,' said three voices firmly, followed by a half-hearted 'agreed' from little Katie.

'Woof,' said Pippa, wagging her tail ferociously.

Just at that moment, the heavens opened and everyone jumped down from Mabel and ran for cover. Emma sprinted as fast as she could down Church Lane.

'Well, Pip,' said Emma, 'as it's raining so hard, let's pop into the church to light a candle for Mum and Dad.' Pippa seemed to nod in reply. Emma's father was in the army so her parents were currently stationed in Cyprus.

Emma glanced around to check no one was watching and then lifted Pippa up and placed her in a shopping bag. They had done this many times before, so Pippa knew to keep still and completely quiet with only her tiny face peeping out.

St Mary Magdalene was a small church, surrounded by a pretty churchyard with an impressive bell tower. Its golden stone always reminded Emma of delicious, crumbly shortbread. A sign on the church gate proudly announced that the church bells were the 'seventh wonder of Wales' and the whole of St David's was extremely proud of them. Emma's grandfather was one of the bell-ringers and had introduced her to all of the bells individually – in his eyes, they each had their own unique character and the bell that was dearest to him was the biggest, Master Thomas.

Emma and Pippa went into the church. The Reverend Pritchard was talking quietly to a parishioner at the front. The inside was beautiful with a ferocious wooden eagle on the pulpit and a rose-stained glass window at the back. However, Emma's favourite part was the set of choir stalls with a carved musical angel adorning each. One angel played a lute while another played the violin and yet another, a harp. For Emma, who had played the piano and sung since early childhood, her favourite angel was the final one who had no instrument and was singing, her eyes lifted heavenwards. 'If I can't become a detective, my ambition is to be a singer,' whispered

Emma to Pippa, 'but I'll probably never be an angel!'

She lit a candle next to the rose window, saying a quick prayer for her absent parents, and turned to leave. As she did so, she bumped into a mother and toddler, whom she didn't know, entering the church. The little girl exclaimed 'Doggy!' loudly on beholding Pippa in the bag. Reverend Pritchard directed a look of consternation towards Emma.

Making a hasty exit, Emma released Pippa to a peal of giggles. 'Oh dear, that little girl's blown our cover.' By this time it had stopped raining, and Emma and Pippa walked back to The Syngret, Emma's grandparents' battered, ivy-covered house, surrounded by garden on all sides.

'Hello, Gramps,' said Emma.

'Hello, my love' said Grandpa, pushing his untidy grey hair off his forehead. 'Did you and that naughty little dog have a good time with your friends?' he asked and smiled his boyish smile.

'Woof,' said Pippa who pirouetted on the spot, chasing her tail.

'Oh yes, thanks, we always do. Gramps, will Mum and Dad come back for the Easter holidays?'

'I don't think so, Red. But I'm sure they'll come back in the summer.'

Emma felt her eyes unexpectedly fill with tears and tried to hide the fact by bending down to stroke Pippa. Her parents had now been in Cyprus for three months and Emma missed her mother, in particular, very much. She was often aware of a pain in her heart, as though a small knife was stuck in her side, but she tried to keep cheerful so as not to upset Edward or her grandparents.

'Still, you'll be talking to them on the telephone tomorrow,' he said. 'That'll be nice, won't it?'

'So I will,' said Emma, trying to smile.

The next day was Sunday and it was raining again. Emma got up early, leaving Pippa snoring on the bed, and practised the piano for half an hour. By this time, everybody was up and drinking tea.

'Really, darling, you know I love to hear you playing the piano,' said Granny, 'but perhaps not quite so early in the morning.'

'Sorry, Granny, I wasn't thinking.'

As usual, they were late for the church service at St Mary Magdalene. Emma rushed up to the choir loft, where she was met with a glance of utmost disapproval from Miss Audrey Prendergast, a formidable lady with lacquered, pewter grey hair, who ruled the choir with a rod of iron. The choir was excellent and had won several local competitions.

On the way out of church, the Reverend Pritchard adjusted his reading glasses and said: 'Ah, Emma, my dear, I see your poodle has not graced us with her presence on this occasion!'

'What on earth did he mean by that?' questioned Granny.

'No idea, Granny,' said Emma, with her most innocent look and her fingers crossed behind her back.

As the service had lasted longer than expected, they rushed home quickly and just got back in time to hear the telephone hooting. It was an unusual Hercule Poirot style candlestick telephone, discovered on one of Grandpa's outings to a junk shop, which he had adapted to sound like an owl.

Pippa was barking excitedly and was urged to quieten down by Granny, while Grandpa answered the telephone.

'Sarah, my dear, lovely to hear your voice,' said Grandpa warmly. 'Yes, we're fine, thank you. The children are looking forward to the Easter holidays. I'll just pass you over to Emma.'

'Mummy, how are you?' asked Emma.

'We're fine,' said Mum. 'Your father's working hard at the army base, but we've made lots of friends. Cyprus is a very friendly place! Are you studying and helping your grandparents?'

'Oh yes, I'm being terribly good.'

At this point, Edward managed to get hold of the telephone. 'Mummy, I'm learning to play the trumpet, just listen to this…' And, placing the receiver on the table, he proceeded to play a few notes down the telephone.

'Stop that at once, Edward,' said Granny, snatching back the telephone. 'Sarah, I'm so sorry, I hope you weren't completely deafened. Your father bought him a trumpet. I can't imagine why!' There was a brief pause as their mother spoke. 'Yes, I know telephoning from Cyprus is expensive. Of course, I understand. Okay, we look forward to speaking to you again soon, we hope.' With that, Granny replaced the receiver.

'Thanks, Ed, for ruining that. I've been dying to speak to Mum all week,' said Emma, looking upset.

'Don't blame, Ed,' said Grandpa, noticing that Edward looked crestfallen. 'He can't help being excited about his trumpet.'

'Children, neither of you has done a stroke of homework all weekend so I suggest you get on with it now,' said Granny tartly. 'And, Edward, it's about time you put Louis Armstrong back in his cage.' She had spotted the little mouse poking out of his pocket.

Emma and Edward sloped off to their bedrooms to get out their schoolbooks, and even Pippa seemed strangely subdued.

Chapter Two

The Detectives Spring Into Action

The following Friday was a dark, dark, moonless night. At 10pm, three slight figures, dressed in black from head to toe, as well as one black poodle, waited anxiously under the oak tree.

'You do think Katie's coming, don't you?' whispered Laurie, tying back her thick dark hair.

'Of course she is,' said Emma. 'She wouldn't let us down.'

Just at that moment, they spotted a small fair-haired figure skirting the edge of the field.

'So sorry I'm late,' said a very out-of-breath Katie. 'Mum seemed to suspect something and kept popping into my bedroom. In the end, I stuffed my pillow and a blanket in my bed so she'd think I was still there, and climbed out of the window. I'll really be in trouble if she finds out.' Katie paused to catch her breath and to reveal an aerosol spray of air freshener. 'I brought this too, to use as a weapon, if need be.'

'Look what I have,' whispered Laurie, showing her torch.

'Here's my camera, in case the villain turns up,' said Emma.

'And I've got a whistle with me,' said Lizzy. They laughed and then told each other to be quiet.

'Now, Pippa,' whispered Emma, 'you must be as quiet as a mouse. Absolutely no barking, you understand?' Pippa nodded solemnly.

They tiptoed across the farmyard and jumped as an owl hooted. As they neared the barn, they heard a few cows making 'mooing' sounds.

'Oh goodness,' said Katie, 'someone's bound to hear us.'

'Ssh,' said the others.

By this time, they had reached the henhouse.

'Shall we check that it really is locked?' said Lizzy.

Emma tried the handle, provoking a few startled gobbling noises from the hens within, but the door was definitely locked.

The girls sat down amongst the bushes, ready for action.

About an hour later, Katie said with a yawn: 'I'm tired and cold. How much longer do you think it's going to be?'

'Real detectives don't give up when the going gets tough, you know,' said Laurie sternly.

At this point, a snore was heard from Pippa.

'Pippa,' whispered Emma, 'you're supposed to be a guard dog!' Pippa opened one eye and sat up sleepily.

'What's that?' asked Lizzy.

They could hear the wheels of a bicycle moving down the lane towards Fairdale farm. Someone got off and leant the bicycle against the wall.

'Oh my goodness, do you think it's the criminal?' whispered Katie in alarm.

'When I give the signal, we'll all pounce,' said Emma. A figure in black, wearing a balaclava, crept closer to the henhouse.

'Supposing he's got a gun?' whispered Katie.

'Nonsense,' said Laurie, looking a little worried in spite of herself.

The figure knelt by the henhouse and took what looked like an extremely long hairpin from his pocket. He carefully inserted it in the lock and moved it left and right. After a few seconds, he managed to unlock the door. At that moment, Emma cried 'Now' and four energetic girls, aided by one exuberant poodle, fell upon the egg thief.

'I surrender, I surrender,' said a frightened boy. 'Get off me!'

Pippa bit his ankle and he gave her a ferocious

kick, sending her flying with a whimper. Emma immediately rushed to her side.

'Pippa, speak to me. Are you all right?' Pippa wagged her tail half-heartedly, but could not put her front paw down on the ground.

'How dare you kick my poodle,' cried Emma fiercely.

Laurie bravely snatched off his balaclava and they beheld Philip Evans, a tall, thin, unpopular boy from the village.

'Philip Evans, what on earth are you doing stealing Farmer Williams' eggs?' asked Emma fiercely.

'Who says I am?' said Philip. 'It's only your word against mine.'

At that point, Emma took a photograph of him standing by the henhouse with the lock pick in his hand. 'I imagine this photo will provide damning evidence,' she said.

'Oh, please don't tell my dad,' cried Philip, all his bravado gone now that he realised he had been caught. 'He'll kill me.' The tears rolled down his beaky nose.

'But why did you do it?' said Katie, opening her blue eyes in wonder.

'Well, it made me extra pocket money when I sold the eggs to the village shop,' Philip explained and sniffed. 'Does anyone have a tissue?'

'Where did you get a lock pick from?' asked Lizzy, raising her eyebrows.

'My uncle had a spare one – it's almost like a party trick, really,' said Philip.

'How extremely irresponsible of him,' cried Laurie.

'Philip Evans, you are a thief and coward as well as a poodle aggressor! Give us one good reason why we shouldn't hand you over to the police immediately,' said Emma sternly.

'Supposing I promise never to do it again?' said Philip.

'I think you should go and confess to Farmer Williams and offer to help him on the farm,' suggested Emma.

'That seems very harsh,' said Philip who sniffled again and wiped his nose on his sleeve.

'No, it doesn't,' said Lizzy coolly.

'Nowhere near harsh enough!' exclaimed Laurie, her dark eyes flashing.

'Does no one have a spare tissue?' sniffed Philip.

'Oh, for heaven's sake, here you are,' said Katie, in exasperation.

At that moment, they heard a car, and a man's voice broke the silence.

'Goodness, who's this?' said Katie.

'Farmer Williams, of course,' said Lizzy.

'Angela, wait there until I find out what's

happening,' said Richard.

The children turned to see Richard walking across the farmyard.

'What on earth's going on?' shouted Richard sternly. 'Good heavens, children, what are you doing here?' he asked in surprise.

'Catching an egg thief red-handed,' said Emma, snatching the lock pick from Philip who started to cry again.

'Philip, is this true?' said Richard, looking stern once again.

'Well, yes,' said Philip, 'but I swear I'll never do it again – only, please don't tell my dad. He'll kill me.'

'Richard, we thought Philip might offer to help you on the farm to make up for everything,' said Emma.

'I can certainly think of a few unpleasant tasks he could help me with,' said Richard grimly. 'Philip, I won't tell the police or your father as long as this never happens again, and if you keep your word to help me on the farm. Let this be a lesson to you.

'And, girls, just think what could have happened if this had been an adult thief, who might have had no qualms about injuring you. Promise me you'll never sneak out in the middle of the night to catch criminals again.'

'One of us has already been injured,' said Emma,

a big tear rolling down her face. By now, she was carrying Pippa. 'This horrible brute has broken Pippa's leg.'

Richard had a look at the sore paw. 'I don't think it's broken, Emma *bach*,' he said. 'Strap it up in a bandage for a few days and I'm sure Pippa will be as right as rain.

'Well then, do you realise that it's past midnight and I'm going to take you home?'

'No, please don't take me,' pleaded Philip. 'My dad can't know anything about this.'

'All right then,' said Richard, 'but I expect you at 8.00am sharp on my farm next Saturday.'

Philip groaned and disappeared as fast as he could.

Now the excitement had worn off, the girls were tired and cold, and Emma was feeling anxious about Pippa's paw.

'Right, get in,' said Richard, gesturing towards his car. 'Have you met Miss Barnard?'

All the girls looked embarrassed as Miss Barnard was an English teacher at Grove Park.

'Okay, I'm going to drop Miss Barnard off first, and then each of you in turn,' said Richard, driving carefully along the silent streets of St David's until he reached Miss Barnard's house.

'Goodnight, Richard and goodnight, girls,' said Miss Barnard, trying to hide a smile at the situation.

'Right then, who lives nearest?' asked Richard.

One by one, Richard delivered the girls to their front doors. The last to be taken home were Emma and Pippa.

'Now, Emma, do you solemnly promise not to do this again?'

'I do, indeed. I'll never forgive myself if Pippa's seriously hurt,' said a subdued Emma, kissing the sleeping poodle in her arms.

'I think she'll be fine,' said Richard kindly.

'You look awfully smart,' said Emma, noticing his black dinner jacket and bow tie.

'Thank you. I've been singing in *Mozart's Requiem* at Old Colwyn Baptist church.'

'Richard, please don't tell my grandparents, will you? They'll only worry.'

'As long as it doesn't happen again, your secret is safe with me,' Richard said with a smile and, with that, Emma and Pippa returned to The Syngret and were soon fast asleep.

The next morning, Emma woke up early, even though she was tired after such a thrilling night.

'Pippa, how's your paw?' Pippa tried to put her paw down, but winced in pain when she did so.

'Gramps, Pippa's hurt her paw and I don't know what to do.'

Grandpa felt her paw and constructed a sling

from a striped red and black scarf. In no time at all, Pippa was hopping around on three legs, looking like a pirate poodle, injured during the course of battle! Then she returned to her basket which was moved to the centre of the living room so that she could be petted to her heart's content.

'Are you okay, Red?' asked Grandpa, looking concerned. 'You look very tired.'

'Yes, darling,' said Granny, 'I do hope you're not coming down with something.'

'I'm fine, thanks,' said Emma. 'I just didn't sleep very well.'

She glanced at the clock and realised she was running late for meeting her friends. She dashed down the lane and across the field to Mabel. Three listless girls were there to greet her.

'I've hardly got the energy to climb Mabel today,' said Katie, but they did, all the same.

'I guess that wasn't the most successful detective work ever,' Lizzy pointed out.

'I disagree,' said Laurie. 'We caught Philip Evans red-handed and, now that we've confiscated his lock pick, he won't be stealing from Farmer Williams or anyone else for that matter! I think we did very well.'

All four girls cheered up at the thought.

'Do you think Miss Barnard is Richard's girlfriend?' wondered Katie.

'No, I'm sure he wouldn't be so silly. I expect he

was just giving her a lift home,' said Emma.

'In my experience,' said Lizzy reflectively, 'grown-ups are always surprisingly silly where romance is concerned!'

'How's Pippa's paw, Emma?' asked Katie, changing the subject.

'Well, as you know, she's a very brave little dog. Grandpa strapped up her paw, and he and Richard think she'll be fine in a couple of days' time. I just hope they're right.'

'That's good news,' said Lizzy.

'Yes, do give her our love,' said Laurie.

'I will, thank you.' Emma smiled. 'My aunt's coming to stay on Monday, so I won't see any of you for a while,' said Emma, already missing her friends.

'Have a lovely time until we meet again.'

'Agreed,' said one and all.

Chapter Three

The Treasure Hunt

On Monday, Auntie Gina and her new husband, David, arrived in their smart red convertible. Auntie Gina was tall, dark-haired and glamorous while David had reddish hair, brown eyes and a warm smile. They were also interesting and great fun. Auntie Gina and David had got married in secret the previous December and honeymooned on the island of Elba over Christmas – so this was the first time they had met, since the wedding. At the time, Emma had been desperately disappointed because Gina had always promised that Emma could be her bridesmaid, and Emma had cried herself to sleep the night she discovered the awful truth, vowing never to speak to Gina again!

They were all soon talking and laughing at once and Pippa was running around, barking excitedly.

'Come into the house,' said Grandpa. 'You must

be starving after the journey.' They trooped into The Syngret, David carrying a huge black case and Gina with two smart, round suitcases in matching shades of pink.

'Gina never did travel light,' said Grandpa with a chuckle.

Neither Grandpa nor Granny was renowned for their domestic skills, so meals often consisted of eggs from Richard's farm, tomatoes from the greenhouse, toast and tea. Grandpa had invented a toaster which played the first line of the Welsh national anthem when the toast popped up!

'Did Richard bring us more eggs?' asked Grandpa. 'I take it the egg problem's resolved then?'

'Yes, apparently so,' said Granny. Emma and Pippa winked at each other, but said nothing.

After the meal, Edward declared excitedly, 'I must play you a tune on my trumpet!' He then rushed off trying hard to remember in which corner he had last left it.

'Your father bought him a trumpet,' said Granny apologetically, raising her eyes to the ceiling.

Edward came back and launched into 'Moon River' which was almost unrecognisable because of the wrong notes. It was also twice as slow as it should have been, and three times as loud. Edward beamed once he had finished and they all applauded.

'Would you like me to play "Climb Every

Mountain" now?' he asked.

'Why don't you save that for another day?' said Granny, diplomatically.

The following morning, the sun was shining, and Gina and David sat around the breakfast table with Emma, Edward and Pippa.

'Children', said Gina, looking serious, but excited. 'We've something to tell you, haven't we, David?'

'Yes,' said David, 'a very strange thing happened last weekend. Gina and I were walking along the beach…'

'…And I happened to notice a glass bottle in the water,' said Gina.

'It was a very old bottle and there was an ancient parchment in it,' added David.

'Would you like to see it?' asked Gina, innocently.

'Yes, please,' said Emma and Edward, and Pippa wagged her tail.

'Here it is, then,' said Gina.

I have roved the seas as a pirate bold,
I have amassed my share of treasure and gold.
My enemies now hold me far, far away
So I send you this message and I gladly say:

My gold is hidden on an isle in the Dee,
Go first to the smallest island of three,
If you are reading this note, it must be fate,
God speed your search, do not tarry or wait!

'Wow,' breathed Edward, his blue eyes like saucers in his face. 'A message from a real pirate. Do you think we can find the treasure?'

'Do we have any idea where the mystery island is?' asked Emma.

'As a matter of fact,' began David, 'I think we do. You see, I was brought up on the Wirral and I know there are three islands on the Dee Estuary: Little Isle, Middle Isle and Holy Isle. The tides around there are deadly – the sea goes a long way out but comes in faster than a galloping horse. But, when the tide's out, you can walk across the sands to the islands.'

'Can we get there without being drowned?' asked Edward.

'Yes, don't worry,' said David.

'I can't wait,' said Edward, clapping his hands together. Pippa barked to show how thrilled she was.

'The only thing is, Emma – I don't think Pippa can come,' said Gina. 'With her sore paw, I don't think she's up to such a long walk.'

'But her paw's much better now,' protested Emma, looking upset. 'She can do it, really she can.'

'That dog is a real trouper,' said Edward.

'Nevertheless,' said Gina, 'I'm afraid we do have to leave her behind.'

'So, tomorrow is D-Day!' said David.

*

The next day, The Syngret was bustling with activity.

'Are you nearly ready?' asked Grandpa.

The red convertible was left open for packing purposes. The boot was not big enough for their rucksacks, which contained their supplies and the all-important picnic, so two were placed on the back seat where Emma and Edward would sit. Pippa was lying in her basket and sulking throughout the preparations.

'I'm sorry, Pippa, but I promise to tell you all about it when we get back,' said Emma, stroking her head.

At that moment, Pippa could bear it no longer and ran off into the garden.

'Never mind, darling,' said Granny. 'She'll get over it.'

'Edward,' said Grandpa. 'What on earth is your trumpet doing in your rucksack?!'

'Well…' Edward began, 'I thought, if the tide should come in galloping like a horse, I could blow my trumpet and someone would rescue us!'

'I admire your forethought,' said David, 'but you can't possibly carry a trumpet all that way.'

'Come on,' urged Gina, 'we need to get a move on so as not to miss low tide.'

The children kissed Granny and Grandpa

farewell. 'Have a wonderful time,' they said.

'Fasten your seat belts,' instructed David, 'and then we'll have lift-off!'

The road ahead was clear, the little car raced along and they sang 'Men of Harlech'. As they got to the end of the song, a rustling sound was heard coming from one of the rucksacks on the back seat.

'What's that?' asked Gina.

At that moment, Pippa's head emerged from the top of the rucksack. She started barking and was clearly laughing at the trick she had played.

'Pippa, you came with us!' squealed Emma, getting her out of the bag and giving her a hug.

'Emma, did you plan this?' asked Gina, sternly.

'No, Auntie Gina. I was upset when you said Pippa couldn't come with us, but I didn't smuggle her on board.'

'What'll we do, David?' said Gina. 'If we turn back now, we'll miss the tide.'

'We'll just have to take that naughty little dog with us and hope she can walk all the way,' said David, trying hard not to smile.

'Hooray,' cheered two children and one poodle.

They parked the car at Kirby, the nearest town to the islands, and walked towards the beach. Silvery water glistened on the sands and they could see the ripples the waves had made when the sea had covered them, just a few hours previously.

'The isles are not as close as you would imagine,' said David. 'This landscape's deceptive and has a haunting, mysterious quality. That's why lots of ghost stories are set on, or near, land sometimes covered by water.'

'In medieval French literature, water is often seen as the gateway between the real world and the fairy kingdom,' said Gina, who had studied French at university.

'Look at those small boats lying lopsided on the sand,' Emma pointed out. 'Don't they look eerie?'

'They'll stand up straight again as soon as the tide comes in,' said Gina.

'Have you heard about the mystery of the Marie Céleste?' asked David.

'No,' answered both Edward and Emma, wide-eyed.

'It was a ship found drifting in the Atlantic towards the end of the nineteenth century and every one of the crew had disappeared. No one's ever discovered what happened. Legend has it that, when the ship was found, the dining table was set for a meal and the food was still warm.'

'What do you think happened?' asked Edward.

'Do either of you have any ideas?' said David.

'Perhaps one of them was a murderer who killed the others, and then killed himself,' said Emma.

'Well,' said Gina, 'my suggestion is that the crew thought the ship was about to sink and took to the lifeboat which was then swept away in a storm and they all drowned.'

'I think they were attacked by pirates and were made to walk the plank!' said Edward, ghoulishly.

'Yes, I'm afraid pirates were not the romantic figures we like to imagine,' said Gina.

'I guess no one will ever know for certain,' said David.

They were now approaching Little Isle. There were several rocks along its side, but the top was a grassy plateau. The long, unmown grass, blown by the wind in one direction, gave the comical effect of backcombed hair.

'Look over there,' said David, pointing. 'Black seaweed. It's really slippery and impossible to cross – and beyond, there's quicksand. That's why it's really important to take the safe route to these islands.'

Gina and David helped the children climb the rocks down to the tiny beach and Pippa managed on her own.

'At high tide, the whole of Little Isle is under water,' said David, as they walked along the beach.

'Where do you think the treasure is?' wondered Emma.

Pippa ran over to a small cave at the end of the

beach and started to bark.

'That's a good idea,' said Emma. 'Let's look inside.'

The cave was about the size of a pantry.

'Look,' said Emma, pointing to a small, waist-high niche. Inside was another parchment, which said:

> *Well done, my hearties, for following this trail,*
> *I wish you luck in your search for the grail!*
> *Go now to the second isle to find the next clue*
> *Entrusted to a mermaid fair, brave and true!*

'I see, this isn't the treasure after all – it's another clue,' said Emma thoughtfully.

'Yes, so we need to go now to Middle Isle,' said Edward. 'Isn't it lucky that we have Captain David with us?'

On the way to Middle Isle, tall, elegant herons turned, from dipping their beaks into rock pools, to stare at them as they passed. A few gulls cried overhead. The sand was becoming less firm in places and one of Edward's Wellington boots got completely stuck in the sand and had to be dug out!

'Can you hear that sound?' asked Emma. 'It's really plaintive.'

'It's the seals,' said Gina. 'Look over there.' They

all turned to see a huge sandbank covered in grey seals.

'Some people think an evil sea witch cast a spell to turn mermaids into seals and that's why they cry – they long to become mermaids once more,' said Gina.

'What's that over there?' asked Edward, almost too distracted to listen.

'I don't know whether it's a trick of the light,' said Gina, 'but it does look as though a golden dog is running towards us.'

They turned to look in the same direction and it then became clear that a golden retriever with shaggy, burnished hair was coming to greet them.

'Hello, you beautiful creature,' said David, stroking the dog's head. He looked at the dog's collar and then said, 'This dog is called Taliesin.'

'Very pleased to meet you, Taliesin,' said Gina, stroking his big head.

Pippa went up to the large dog and they both sniffed each other's noses suspiciously for a while. They then wagged their tails furiously as they had clearly decided to become friends.

'Where are your humans?' said David.

'I don't see anyone,' said Gina. 'So, Taliesin, you're very welcome to come along with us.'

Pippa barked encouragement while Taliesin nodded sagely. By this time, they were approaching

Middle Isle. The second island was rockier than the first with cockles and barnacles sticking to the rocks. Steep steps led up to a path winding across the top of the island to the red cliffs at the far end.

'Just look at the view,' cried Gina.

'It's amazing,' said Emma, and the dogs barked in unison.

'You can see as far as Mount Snowdon,' said David.

'Please can we stay here always?' asked Edward.

'You might not like it so much in a howling gale!' said Gina, before laughing merrily.

'We're enjoying the journey so much,' said Emma, 'we've forgotten to look for the next clue!'

'As you will recall, it was "entrusted to a mermaid",' Gina reminded them.

'Do you think it could be on that sandbank over there with the seals?' said Edward.

'Oh I see, because of the myth of mermaids becoming seals? Good thinking, Ed, but I guess not, because the last clue definitely directed us towards this island. Why don't we consult your map, David?' said Gina.

They knelt down on the cliffs and unfolded the map, with the dogs standing guard.

'Look,' said Emma, pointing. 'There's a Mermaid's Cove just by these cliffs, but how do we get down there?'

'Over here,' called Gina. 'There are steps down to the beach.'

'Okay, everyone, we need to be really careful,' warned David. 'I'll go first so, if any of you trip, you can fall on me!' They gingerly made their way down to the sand.

'But now what?' said Edward.

'Why don't we explore and see whether anywhere looks like a suitable hiding place?' said Gina.

Emma went to the far end of the beach where a large rock was located. As she looked at it, she suddenly realised what it was.

'I've found the mermaid!' she shouted and they came dashing over. 'Look, this is her face, here's her arm and the bottom part's her swishy fish tail!' exclaimed Emma.

'Can any of you see the next clue?' said David.

They circled the rock and Edward shouted, 'There's something in the sand.'

David started digging and found an old-fashioned sweet tin. It opened to reveal another parchment, folded up tightly inside. It read:

Very impressive, hats off, ahoy!
To get this far must give you great joy.
For the treasure itself, climb a very great height,
It is safe in the path of a bright beam of light.

'Gosh,' said Emma, 'but do we know where we're going next?'

'I think there can be no doubt,' said Gina. 'We need to walk to Holy Isle.'

'Follow me, comrades,' said David, and with that, the brave and merry little troupe marched on behind him.

'Edward, your nose is looking red. Let me put suntan lotion on it,' suggested Gina. As she stooped down, a gust of wind swept her sun hat into the air and deposited it into a nearby rock pool. They all laughed. David fished it out for her.

'I'm glad it isn't made of straw,' said Gina, 'so, luckily, it'll dry. And, prepared as always like the good Girl Guide I used to be, I have another with me.' With a flourish, she produced a replacement floppy hat from her rucksack.

They were now drawing near to Holy Isle. It looked so beautiful as they walked towards it in silence.

'What're those old buildings over there?' said Edward.

'This was a busy trading port during the 1550s,' said David. They climbed up the mossy steps to the main street.

'Do be careful, children,' said Gina. 'And dogs,' she added as Taliesin's paw slipped on a slimy step.

'What does that sign say?' said Emma.

'It's Seagull Inn,' said Gina. 'Do you know what an "inn" is?'

'Yes,' said Edward, 'it's where grown-ups get drunk and do silly things.'

'That's a very good description, Ed,' said David.

They peeked inside. 'When this was a busy port, can you imagine what the inn would have been like on a Saturday night?' asked David. 'There would have been drunks and people would have been laughing, playing cards and gambling. There also would have been people trying to sell smuggled goods and perhaps the odd fight or two.'

'Do you think our pirate would've been one of them?' said Emma.

'Possibly,' said Gina, 'and I'm sorry to say there would also have been wreckers.'

'What are wreckers?' asked Edward.

'Some wicked people lured ships to their doom by standing on rocks waving a lantern to and fro. This led the sailors to believe the light was another ship and the waters were safe. But when boats sailed nearer, they broke up on the rocks, the people on board drowned and the wreckers stole everything they could lay their hands on. That's how they made their living.'

The children looked shocked.

'Ah, the world is new to thee,' said Gina, with

a sad smile.

'But that's so wicked,' shouted Edward. 'It's murder.'

'Calm down,' said David. 'Though, you're quite right, of course.'

'Anyway, I'm starving,' said Edward. 'Can we stop and eat?'

'Yes, we'll have a picnic over there,' said Gina, pointing to a grassy patch on the cliff with a fantastic view out to sea.

They sat down on the ground and brought out food and drink. Gina had a plastic bowl, which the dogs shared amicably. Nothing could be heard for a while except for gulls crying, and humans and dogs munching.

Gina finished eating first and, while waiting for the rest to finish, recited a verse:

'Be not afeard; the isle is full of noises,
Sounds and sweet airs, that give delight and hurt not.
Sometimes a thousand twangling instruments
Will hum about mine ears, and sometime voices
That, if I then had waked after long sleep,
Will make me sleep again.'

'Is that a famous poem?' said Emma.
'Or did you just make it up?' said Edward.
'No, darling, I'm not Shakespeare!' exclaimed

Gina. 'It's from his last play *The Tempest*, which is set on an island.'

'Is Pippa all right?' asked David. 'Her head's between her paws.'

'Oh yes,' said Emma, 'she's just cat napping.' At the word 'cat', Pippa opened one eye and looked up.

'Let's be on our way then,' said David. They started to walk across the island.

'What's the building over there?' wondered Edward.

'There were Benedictine monks here for four hundred years,' stated David, 'and that was the chapel. You can see the monks' tombstones in the graveyard over here.'

'In horror films,' continued Gina, 'graveyards are scary places but, in real life, they're often beautiful and peaceful.'

'It's been so interesting,' said Emma, 'we've almost forgotten the treasure!'

'What did the clue say, again?' said Edward.

'Climb a very great height,' said Gina. 'It's safe in the path of a bright beam of light.'

'Of course, it's the lighthouse,' said Emma, jumping up and down in excitement. 'Look ahead of you.'

They were starting to tire but, now with the treasure within grasp, they picked up their pace towards the impressive, white lighthouse.

'It must be right at the top,' said Edward, 'if we need to climb.'

'Let's hope the door's unlocked,' said David, and it was.

The children were too excited to speak and climbed the winding staircase in solemn silence. Finally, they reached the topmost room where the powerful beam was located. The room had incredible three hundred and sixty degree views over the sea; the Wirral to the east and North Wales to the west. There was a telescope, looking out to sea, and a trunk Edward climbed onto in order to look through it.

'That's it,' said Emma excitedly.

The others stared at her. 'What?'

'The treasure must be in the trunk,' said Emma. 'Get down, Edward.'

David tried the lid of the trunk, but it was locked.

'We need the key,' said Gina, 'but where can it be?'

The only piece of furniture in the room was a mahogany desk with a tiny drawer. Emma opened it and there, on a piece of black velvet, was a small brass key.

'Why don't you try the key in the lock, Ed?' said Gina.

Edward took the key without a word, as though aware of his great responsibility, and tried it in the lock. It opened and he lifted up the lid. Inside, they found a pirate's costume for Edward with a toy parrot to fix on his shoulder. For Emma, there was a golden bracelet with charms of a mermaid, an anchor, a ship, and a skull and crossbones. There were also lots of chocolate gold coins for everyone.

'How wonderful,' cried the children, dancing around in delight, and both dogs wagged their tails.

'Look, the pirate's last message is at the bottom of the trunk,' said Gina.

This treasure is yours – I hope you are pleased.
You deserve it greatly for your heroic deeds.
Through life's adventure, let not riches enthral,
Try to remember that the journey is all.

'I hate to be a party pooper,' said Gina, 'but I think we ought to start heading back. We need to go before the tide comes in.'

'Of course, Auntie Gina,' said the children, putting their treasure away carefully in their rucksacks.

They climbed down the stairs and started to walk back.

As they left the island, Edward turned and said, 'Farewell, most beautiful Holy Isle.' And they all waved goodbye.

After all the excitement, and the long walk in the wind and sun, everyone started to feel tired and wish they were back home. More worryingly, Pippa started to limp.

'I must say, Pippa,' said Gina, 'I don't have much sympathy. We did tell you to stay at home.'

They carried on walking. After a while, David suddenly said, 'Where's Emma?' They all looked back in concern. They saw Emma had lagged behind and was carrying Pippa. David walked back to join her. 'That's very valiant of you, Emma, but I know that poodle is heavier than she looks.' With that, he took Pippa from Emma.

'She'd be easier to carry on your back,' said Gina, so they distributed the contents of David's rucksack between them and Pippa sailed along on David's back with her little face peeping out.

'That poodle may as well be the Queen of Sheba,' added Gina tartly.

'She's the best poodle in the world,' said Emma defensively.

'Of that, there is no doubt,' said David.

And the not-so-merry little troupe walked on, and the return journey seemed a lot longer than the outgoing one had been.

As they arrived at the steps back up to the prom, Edward turned and said, 'I'll remember this day always, for as long as I live.'

Gina and David looked moved, and Gina kissed the top of his head. 'You've been such a good boy, Ed, and I know it's been a very long way for you.'

'Oh my goodness, what're we going to do about Taliesin!?' Emma suddenly exclaimed.

'Yes, we never did find your humans, did we?' said David.

'I'll just look at his name tag again,' said Gina. 'Phew, what a relief! His address is the Sea Shanty café, just along the prom. I don't know about you, but I'm dying to sit down and have a cup of tea, in any case.'

They walked along the prom to the café. As they entered, the large, fair-haired woman, who owned the café, smiled and said, 'Taliesin, have you been over to the isles again?' Mrs Richards bore a striking resemblance to her dog!

'Yes, we're bringing him back to you. He joined us on our journey,' said David.

'He loves those islands,' said Mrs Richards, stroking his majestic head, 'and goes there as often as he can.'

They sat drinking tea and admiring the café. It was wooden and painted light blue with a ceiling in the shape of the bottom of a sailing boat.

Everyone was tired and Edward fell asleep with his head on the table.

'It was a pleasure to have you with us, Taliesin,'

said Gina, and the dog held out his paw to be shaken by each of them in turn.

'I feel sure we'll meet again,' said Emma.

They said goodbye to Mrs Richards and made their way to the car. The sun was setting behind Holy Isle, and their last view was of the isles bathed in glorious gold, orange and red.

Chapter Four

In Praise of Myfanwy

The following Saturday, Lizzy, Laurie and Katie were already at the foot of Mabel, the apple tree, and waved when they saw Emma coming across the field.

Emma told them about the great Treasure Hunt, and they were enchanted. She also showed them her charm bracelet.

'That's really wonderful,' said Katie.

'You'll remember it always,' enthused Laurie.

'You do realise that your aunt and uncle devised the whole thing for you and Edward?' said Lizzy thoughtfully. 'Perhaps they wanted to give you a special adventure to remember. It's a remarkable gift.'

'Yes, I tried to believe they'd really discovered a message in a bottle, but reason got the better of me,' said Emma. 'Please don't tell Edward though – he'd be very disappointed.'

'Of course not,' they said.

'That's a lovely bracelet,' said Lizzy, 'but as the final message says, "it's as nothing in comparison with the journey you made".'

'Guess who I saw last Saturday?' said Katie, chuckling. 'Philip Evans, looking miserable and cleaning out Farmer Richard's cowshed.' They all laughed.

'Serves him right!' said Laurie with a curl of her lip.

'And talking of Farmer Richard,' said Katie. 'I saw him collect Miss Barnard in his car after work.'

'So it really does look as though she's his girlfriend,' said Lizzy with a smile.

'Yes, sorry, Emma,' added Katie.

'I can't imagine why any of you would think that the romantic shenanigans of Farmer Williams could possibly interest me in the slightest,' said Emma, at her most highty-toighty and using her poshest accent.

'Well, you may not be on a very high branch,' said Lizzy acerbically, 'but you certainly seem to have got on your high horse!'

'Oh, let's have a game of "What's the time, Mr Wolf?"' said Emma in her normal voice, and that's what they did.

A neighbour had given Grandpa a dinghy with a

broken motor, and trying to fix it now became Grandpa's consuming passion. During this period, he became 'grumpy Gramps' as he was increasingly exasperated by not being able to repair the engine.

After almost a whole day of banging and hammering, followed by endless revving to no avail, Granny lost her temper. 'I don't know which is worse, your engine or Edward's trumpet!' She took her sketching pad into the caravan and slammed the door shut.

The rest of the Easter holidays whizzed by in a flash and then it was time for school again. The girls were soon absorbed by the rhythm of school and the summer term passed quickly, dominated by revision and exam nerves. All of them did well, and Miss Prendergast and the school choir came top in another choral competition.

The last day of the summer term was soon upon them. In the assembly hall, everyone sang the school song 'Days of Glory' with more zeal than usual with Miss Prendergast at the piano. Afterwards, lots of excited girls shrieked and chattered, hugging and waving each other goodbye and happy holidays until the autumn term.

As the friends made their way home along the river, Emma threw her straw boater into the air and cried, 'Hooray, no more school for two whole months, and no more Miss Grigson ever again, with any luck.'

'As long as none of us is foolish enough ever to take needlework,' said Katie.

They all fell on the grass under one of the horse-chestnuts and laughed until they could laugh no more.

'Aren't we horrible,' said Katie. 'But there's only so much of your form teacher you can take.'

'Wonder who we'll have the pleasure of next year,' said Lizzy.

'Don't know. Don't care. It's the holidays now,' said Emma. 'Can't wait to see Mum and Dad. They'll be back in a few weeks.'

'That's good,' said Laurie, 'and in time for your birthday too.'

'Yes, it'll be marvellous. Let's hope it's a good summer and we can spend as much time as possible on the beach,' said Emma.

'We're so lucky that we live close to the sea,' said Lizzy. 'See you all tomorrow,' she said, turning into the driveway of her house. Katie and Laurie also waved goodbye when they reached the centre of the village.

'See you tomorrow,' said Emma, who had further to walk to reach The Syngret. On her way, she had to pass 'the Splash', the village pond where swans swam gracefully and ducks quacked merrily.

As she turned into the drive of The Syngret, Grandpa came rushing out of the garage, his blue eyes sparkling.

'Great news, Red!' he cried. 'I've got Myfanwy going.'

'Who's Myfanwy and where's she going?' asked Emma in puzzlement.

'The boat, of course. Just listen to this...' Grandpa ushered her into the garage, turned the key in the ignition and, with a splutter, the engine sprang to life. 'At last, after all my hard work, she's finally going. I almost gave up several times, but she's a great little boat,' said Grandpa, proudly.

'That's wonderful, Gramps. Well done!' Pippa ran out of the house to bark her congratulations. Just at that moment, Granny stepped out of the caravan looking amazed.

'Is that a running engine I can hear?' she asked in astonishment. 'Oh, Ernest, how clever you are. I shouldn't have doubted you for a moment.' She gave him a kiss, which made Emma feel embarrassed. She pretended to look in her satchel. 'I believe this calls for a bottle of my elderflower champagne,' said Granny.

'Do you think that's wise?' asked Grandpa.

'It isn't that alcoholic.' She went down into the cellar and came back, brandishing a bottle. 'Unfortunately, all the rest have exploded,' she said ruefully. 'So this is the last one. I'll put it in the fridge to cool.'

'Where's Edward?' asked Emma.

'Oh, he's in the garden, pretending to be a bat,' said Granny, vaguely.

'A what?' asked Emma, and she went to have a look. She found Edward at the end of the garden. Grandpa had given him his old black gabardine to cut up, and Edward had made a hole for his head, and was holding the sides of it and swooping about.

'What're you doing, Edward?' asked Emma.

'It's the cub scouts' gala next Tuesday and we have to go in fancy dress. Do I look like a bat?'

'I tell you what, we'll make you a bat mask tomorrow and then you will,' said Emma kindly. 'Amazingly, Gramps has managed to get the boat's engine running and he's named her Myfanwy.'

'Wow. He must be the best grandpa in the whole of Wales.'

'In the whole of the world, Edward,' corrected Emma.

'Children, it's time for tea,' called Granny.

So, on this celebratory occasion, the elderflower champagne was opened to accompany their eggs and toast. Grandpa took the bottle outside to remove the cork, which made the loudest possible pop and flew into the rose bush.

'My goodness, it's potent stuff,' said Grandpa.

'Now, children, you can have a little drop to taste,' said Granny, 'but your grandfather and I will share the rest.'

'Here's a toast to Myfanwy, the best boat in north Wales,' said Grandpa.

'To Myfanwy,' they said and clinked their glasses together.

'There's a song called 'Myfanwy' in my trumpet book,' said Edward 'I'll play it in honour of the occasion. The only thing is, I don't know it very well, so it won't be up to my usual standard.' They looked at each other. He started playing and, with the best will in the world, no one was able to recognise the tune.

'Well, as a sight-reading exercise, it was very promising,' said Grandpa, and everyone agreed that much progress had been made.

Granny whispered in Grandpa's ear and started to giggle. 'You naughty girl,' said Grandpa flirtatiously.

'Okay,' announced Emma. 'Ed and I'll just clear the table, wash up and go to bed.'

Granny pealed with laughter again. The children were non-plussed and started clearing away as fast as they could.

'Would you like me to make coffee?' said Emma.

'No, no,' said Granny. 'We haven't finished the elderflower champagne yet.'

The children's hearts sank and Pippa shook her head.

'Edie, what about a little dancing?' asked Grandpa.

'That'd be wonderful,' agreed Granny, eyes shining. Grandpa started rolling up the carpet. 'Now, where did I put the gramophone? Ah yes, I was repairing it so it's probably in the garage.'

'What's a gramp-o-phone?' said Edward.

'It's an old-fashioned record player in a wooden box with a wind-up handle,' explained Grandpa. 'Its speaker looks a bit like a trumpet. You'll see, Ed, if I can find it.'

'I'll put my dancing shoes on,' said Granny.

'Goodnight then,' said Emma and Edward, as they climbed the stairs with Pippa following and Louis Armstrong tucked into Edward's pocket.

In the style of most of Grandpa's contraptions, the wooden 1940s record-player took time to get started but, when it finally did, The Syngret was filled with the strains of Glenn Miller at full throttle. Emma tried to read a book as a distraction, since she couldn't sleep. An hour later, Edward appeared at her door. The buttons on his pyjamas were done up incorrectly.

'How long do you think they're going to keep this up?' asked Ed.

'Difficult to predict, I'd say,' replied Emma. Pippa looked at her. 'Okay, I'll talk to them.'

She went downstairs and caught a glimpse of Grandpa and Granny smooching across the floor, totally absorbed in each other and the music. Emma knocked on the open door.

'Granny, Gramps, could you possibly turn the music down a bit?' asked Emma. 'We can't get to sleep.'

Neither Grandpa nor Granny reacted in any way. In fact, it was doubtful that they had even heard her, so lost were they in the sounds of their youth. Emma shrugged her shoulders and went back upstairs.

'What's happening?' asked Edward.

'Don't ask,' said Emma. 'I've got an idea though.' She went into the bathroom and placed cotton wool buds, first in Edward's ears, then in Pippa's, and finally in her own. In this way, they finally got to sleep.

The following day, no one got up early. At 9am Emma awoke and went to find Edward, leaving Pippa snoring on the bed. He was just getting dressed. They went downstairs. The carpet was still rolled up; the gramophone was on the table; as was the empty bottle of elderflower champagne.

'It's probably a merciful release the other bottles exploded,' said Emma.

'Just shows how dangerous elderflower champagne can be,' said Edward, solemnly.

They went into the kitchen and made breakfast. Emma then helped Edward to make his bat mask.

'Do you realise it's ten thirty and there's no sign of them?'

'You don't think they died in the night, do you?' said Edward, looking upset.

'No, Edward, I don't think one bottle of elderflower champagne can kill you. I'll go and find out.'

Emma went upstairs but, if truth be told, felt nervous about what she might find. She knocked on the door of her grandparents' room.

'Granny, Gramps, are you okay?' she said, gently opening the door. She was met with groans from both.

'I've got the most terrible headache,' said Granny.

'And my back's extremely painful,' added Grandpa.

'Would you like me to open the curtains?' asked Emma, brightly.

'On no account!' exclaimed Granny sharply.

'Absolutely not,' said Grandpa.

'Emma, darling, would you be an angel and fetch some aspirin and ice for my head?' said Granny with her eyes closed.

'And could you also manage some tea and a hot

water bottle for my back?' asked Grandpa.

'Cinderella's at your service!' cried Emma. She smiled ruefully and went back downstairs.

'Are they okay?' asked Edward anxiously.

'They're a bit the worse for wear but they'll live. My services are needed to get them on their feet, so there's no Mabelling for me this morning. Edward, please could you go and tell my friends that Granny and Gramps are… indisposed, so I can't join them this morning? You can take Pippa along, if you like.'

'Will do,' said Edward, obligingly.

With Emma's help, Grandpa and Granny managed to get up in time for the afternoon, both looking a little tired and pale.

'Thank you, darling,' said Granny. 'It's unusual for me to get such a bad migraine.'

'Yes, Granny,' said Emma, and Pippa raised her eyes heavenwards!

The next day was Sunday and the family went to the golden, crimbly-crumbly church for the service. Emma climbed up to the choir loft, and Miss Prendergast smiled benignly as, for once, Emma was on time. When they were back home later, Emma heard the telephone owl hooting and quickly came downstairs to speak to her parents. She noticed that Granny was looking serious. 'Of course, you must do as you think best, but I can't pretend it isn't a huge disappointment and it'll be very upsetting for the children.' She pursed her lips and handed the telephone over to Emma.

'Mummy, how lovely to hear your voice,' said Emma.

'Fantastic news about your exam results,' said Mum. 'You're such a clever girl. And I hear the choir came first again. Well done, my darling.'

'Thanks very much. When're you arriving, Mummy?' said Emma excitedly. 'Ed and I are dying to see you.'

'Emma, I'm so sorry but we can't come this summer. Your father's been given charge of army manoeuvres and his leave's been cancelled. This is a disappointment for you and Edward, but I know you'll be my big, brave girl. It's a real blow to us too.'

'But can't we fly out to see you and Dad instead? I thought the army paid for family visits.'

'I really don't think that'd be a good idea. You know how fair-skinned you and Edward are. The temperature goes up to forty degrees centigrade here and the sun's blazing. In fact, your father and I spend every weekend in a beautiful village, Pedhoulas, up in the mountains where it's cooler. You and Ed would have to stay inside in the air-conditioning all the time. You'll have a much happier and healthier time in north Wales for the holidays and the months will pass really quickly until the autumn half-term, or possibly Christmas.'

'I don't believe you want to see us!' shouted Emma angrily and dropped the telephone receiver. She burst into tears and rushed out.

Granny picked up the receiver and said gravely, 'You can hardly blame the girl, Sarah. Yes, goodbye for now.' She wiped a tear from her own eye and went to tell Grandpa.

While Granny went to break the news to Edward, Grandpa looked for Emma. He found her sobbing in the caravan, as though her heart would break.

'Dearest Red,' he said. 'I'm so sorry. Life doesn't always go the way we would like. I wish it did.'

'They don't love us,' said Emma, crying into his shirt as he patted her head.

'Yes they do, Emma *bach*.'

He let her cry until she was exhausted.

'There's my best girl – after Myfanwy, of course,' said Grandpa, with a twinkle in his eye.

Emma tried to smile, wiped her red eyes, and they went into the greenhouse to pick tomatoes.

The next day, Granny and Grandpa decided to take the children into Colwyn. They loved furniture auctions, despite the fact they could rarely afford to buy anything. They went first to Peacock's auction rooms on the High Street.

'What a beautiful cupboard thing, Granny,' said Edward.

'Yes, it's a Welsh dresser and that's a particularly fine example,' said Granny.

'And look at this little grandfather clock,' said Emma.

'Actually, it's a grandmother clock! They look like grandfather clocks except they're much smaller,' explained Granny.

'Come and see this flame-haired mermaid,' said Grandpa, his eyes gleaming. 'She'd look fantastic on the prow of Myfanwy.'

'I'm not sure that a dinghy has a prow,' said Granny.

'What's a prow?' asked Edward.

'It's the front part of a boat.'

'So, Myfanwy's a mermaid,' said Emma, 'but I guess we don't really want her to go under water!'

The auction was about to start so they went into the auction room. The auctioneer was a smartly dressed man at the front. He started with a low price for each item and bidders raised their hands to offer increased prices. The piece of furniture was sold to the highest bidder.

'Granny,' whispered Edward. 'What's that wooden hammer?'

'It's called a gavel and the auctioneer bangs it to

indicate when each piece has been sold,' whispered Granny by way of explanation.

There were no other bidders for Grandpa's mermaid, so he got her for a bargain price. At the end of the auction, Grandpa went to pay and then placed the mermaid in the boot of Major Beetroot, their battered, dark red car.

'Now, let's go and have tea and cakes,' said Granny. 'I know The Welsh Room's expensive but I do love it!'

The Welsh Room was a charmingly old-fashioned tea room on the sea-front with waitresses, dressed in traditional Welsh costume, and a harpist in the corner. It also had wonderful melt-in-the-mouth cakes.

'It's incredible that Welsh women really wore that costume in the nineteenth century,' said Granny. 'Those hats seem so inconvenient.'

'They look like witches' hats,' said Edward in wonder.

'It's such luck that we came to the auction today,' said Grandpa. 'Or else, I would never have found the mermaid. It must be fate. I'm going to paint Myfanwy blue to match the mermaid's eyes.'

They chose different cakes and licked their lips when they saw them. They cut them into four pieces so that they could have a taste of each. Edward got cream all over his mouth and fingers and Granny passed him a paper napkin. 'That was delicious,' declared Emma.

As they were leaving, a woman, who was just emerging from a hairdresser's across the street, hailed Granny gleefully.

'Edith, darling, how lovely to see you. It's been an age.'

'Hello, Cynthia, how are you? Yes, we don't seem to have bumped into each other at church recently.'

'Probably because we arrange the flowers on different days.' Cynthia laughed affectedly. 'Well, I'm absolutely fine, thank you, Edith. You're looking rather pale and tired. Are these your grandchildren? My goodness, it must be challenging looking after them at your time of life, and I believe you had a heart scare too last year, didn't you, Ernest?' said Cynthia merrily.

'Thanks for your concern, Cynthia, but I'm as fit as a flea now,' said Grandpa firmly.

'Yes, and we love having them actually,' said Granny.

'How noble of you. Still, I expect their parents will be coming back any day for the summer holidays, won't they?' said Cynthia.

'Well...' Granny hesitated. 'Their plans aren't quite finalised yet.'

'Oh dear,' tittered Cynthia. 'I seem to have touched on a sensitive subject. All the best dear. I'll have to go now as I'm meeting Roger in the Welsh Room. Next time you're coming to Colwyn, do give me a ring – we can meet up for coffee and a proper chinwag.' And she rushed off to meet her husband.

'That woman is insufferable,' said Grandpa heatedly.

'Yes, dear, she always was,' said Granny. 'Actually, I hear that Roger's antique business is going under, so that must be very stressful. Maybe that's why Cynthia's even more unpleasant than usual.'

'Don't make excuses for her, Edie,' said Grandpa. 'She's just a phoney, nasty piece of work.'

'Why is that lady's hair blue? I think it's horrible,' said Edward and they laughed.

Unfortunately, the poisonous encounter with Cynthia left them feeling deflated and everyone was quiet on the way home. When they got back, Emma went to find Granny.

'Granny,' said Emma, looking a little uncertain as to how to begin.

'Yes, dear, what is it?'

'I was just wondering about what the delightful Cynthia was saying… are we too much for you and Gramps? It would be awful if we made you ill. I think the army pays for boarding schools. I could board at Grove Park, and Edward could go to St

David's. Of course, Pippa couldn't actually go to boarding school,' she added, trying to sound more light-hearted. 'So perhaps she could stay here with you?'

'My darling girl,' said Granny, giving her a big hug. 'I meant every word I said to that woman. We love having you (Pippa included). Your grandfather and I have taken on a new lease of life with you in the house.'

'Do you really think so?' asked Emma anxiously.

'Yes and I promise to let you know if we ever get too old or ill to look after you.'

'Thanks very much, Granny,' said Emma, quietly.

'And I, for one, have no intention of giving any more thought to the dreaded Cynthia. You can't let vultures make you unhappy.'

'You're quite right, Granny. I think I'll go and take Pippa for a walk,' said Emma.

Granny was looking pensive, as she watched Emma leave.

Chapter Five

The Vanishing Teapot

The following Friday evening, Grandpa was getting ready for bell-ringing practice. Emma said, 'Gramps, can I come with you? I'd love to listen and I won't be a nuisance, I promise.'

'Of course, Red. We'd be delighted to have you. You can sit in the church and listen. There's only just enough room for the six of us in the ringing chamber.'

They set off together down Church Lane towards St Mary Magdalene. It was a beautiful summer evening and a few hippety-hoppety rabbits nibbled at the grass in Mabel's field, but ran off as soon as they saw Emma and Grandpa. As they reached the church door, Farmer Richard was just arriving with Miss Barnard.

'Hello, Ernest... and Emma, you've come, too,' said Richard warmly.

'Yes, Gramps said I could sit in the church and listen,' explained Emma. 'Hello, Miss Barnard, I didn't know you were a bell-ringer.'

'I'm not sure I can claim to be a bell-ringer,' said Miss Barnard with a smile. 'I'm a complete novice but Richard is a very good teacher.'

While they were talking, Ernest unlocked the church. Being the church warden he had his own key. At this moment, two more bell-ringers arrived: Lizzy's father, Peter Jones, and Cynthia's husband, Roger Rogers.

'Welcome, everyone,' said Ernest. 'Now is anyone missing?'

'Yes, Colonel Granger isn't here yet,' said Richard.

'I do hope he comes soon. We're supposed to start at seven o'clock and it's already ten past. I'm afraid I have to leave at eight sharp as Kay and I are going out to dinner,' said Peter Jones. 'It's our wedding anniversary, you see,' he added bashfully.

'Congratulations,' they said, and Roger clapped him on the back.

'Well, do you think we should go upstairs and see how far we can get without him?' asked Richard.

'There isn't much point, though, is there?' said Grandpa. 'We really need all six bells in action at once. It's a bit much for him to keep us waiting like this.'

Just then, Colonel Granger strode up to the

church, carrying a huge holdall. He was the only one wearing a three-piece suit.

'Good evening one and all. Sorry I'm late but urgent affairs kept me in the office until now,' he bellowed. 'Not that I begrudge it, of course, when my work is of such importance to the community at large,' he added officiously.

At this, Grandpa bit his lip and Richard tried not to smile too broadly.

'Well, at least you're here now,' said Peter rather pointedly. 'I have to leave at eight sharp. It's my wedding anniversary.'

'Of course,' said Colonel Granger. 'Delighted to hear that some of us have time for frivolity! Why don't the rest of you go up to the ringing chamber? I'll just wash my hands and then join you.'

Emma sat in the church next to her beloved choir stall angels and, shortly afterwards, the bells began to ring. It seemed to her that the sound was like a magical fountain, gushing silver and golden water. At eight o'clock, the bell ringers climbed down the wooden steps from the ringing chamber on the first floor.

'That seemed to go well,' said Roger.

'Yes, I do feel that I'm starting to get the hang of it,' said Miss Barnard.

'Well, I must dash,' said Peter. 'See you next week,' and Roger waved goodbye, as well.

'Actually, I must make haste, too,' declared Colonel Granger. 'Some of us need to go back to the office, you know. After that, I have to drive to Birmingham on business.' He rushed off, brandishing his holdall.

'What does he do that's so important?' asked Richard in amusement.

'Well, he was in the army before he retired but he's now a Conservative councillor,' said Grandpa. 'Of course, no one else thinks that's quite as important as he does!'

They all laughed.

'Did you like the bell-ringing, Emma?' asked Richard.

'I loved it,' said Emma enthusiastically. 'It's almost as good as your singing!'

'See you soon, then,' said Richard, and Angela waved goodnight.

'Emma, I just need to oil the church gate – it won't take a moment and then we'll be off home,' said Grandpa.

'That's fine with me, Gramps. It's such a lovely evening, I'll go and say hello to Mabel.'

When Emma returned, Gramps smiled and moved the gate to and fro. 'Listen, Emma, not a squeak now. Reverend Pritchard has just popped into the vestry. Let's say goodnight to him before we go.'

They went back into the church and stopped in alarm when they saw the Reverend Pritchard sitting at the desk with his head in his hands.

'Father Pritchard,' said Grandpa, 'is something wrong?'

'Oh, Ernest,' cried Reverend Pritchard, clearly in distress. 'You'll never believe what's happened. All the money the parish has saved for repairing the church roof has gone.'

'Are you sure?' asked Ernest. 'How much was it and where did you keep it?'

'I'm ashamed to admit there was nearly £1,000 in the large blue teapot in my cupboard,' said the Reverend Pritchard, looking very red in the face, and showing them the cupboard.

'Well, might you have put it somewhere else instead or locked it away?' asked Emma innocently, while Grandpa pressed her arm meaningfully.

'No, that's definitely where I kept it!' cried Reverend Pritchard and he put his head in his hands again.

'Look, the best thing is for me to telephone the police,' said Grandpa.

Constable Roberts arrived quickly in his patrol car and they explained the situation to him.

'So, let me get this straight, Reverend,' said Constable Roberts. 'Nearly £1,000 was kept in the large blue teapot in your cupboard. Did you lock the cupboard?'

'No,' said the Reverend Pritchard weakly. 'And did you ever lock the vestry?' he added. At this, the Reverend Pritchard looked as though he might burst into tears.

'The vestry isn't locked but the church is always locked at six,' said Grandpa. 'It'd be very difficult for someone to sneak into the vestry during the day without being seen.'

'Father, can you remember when you last saw the teapot?' asked Constable Roberts, trying not to sound exasperated.

'Well, I definitely saw it this morning – or I suppose it might have been yesterday,' said Reverend Pritchard. 'I know this must seem really irresponsible but it never occurred to me that anyone would think of stealing the money. How foolish I am!' he added and blew his nose loudly.

'Well, I'll be back tomorrow,' said Constable Roberts, 'to test for fingerprints.'

'You can rest assured, Constable,' said Reverend Pritchard, 'that, in future, I'll always lock away money and valuables.' Neither Grandpa nor Constable Roberts liked to point out that this resolution was too late to save the church's roof repair fund.

'Well, at least no one was hurt and there's been

no damage to the church itself,' said Grandpa, trying to look on the bright side. 'Try not to feel too upset,' he added.

'See you on Sunday, Father,' said Emma.

Grandpa and Emma walked pensively back to The Syngret.

'What's wrong?' said Granny, when they got back. 'Did bell-ringing go badly?'

Grandpa explained the situation and then Granny, too, looked distressed.

'Oh dear,' she said. 'This is much worse than Richard's egg situation. Who would think of stealing from a church?'

'The worst of it is, Edie, that the thief's very likely to be someone in the village. A complete stranger going into the vestry during the day would have been noticed. It's really awful.'

Emma felt guilty about feeling so excited over this new case for investigation when her grandparents and Reverend Pritchard were so upset about it. As soon as she got into her bedroom, she picked up Pippa and waltzed about the room.

'Oh, Pippa, we have a juicy, new case to solve. It's bound to test our powers far more than the egg mystery did!' she cried.

Emma felt as though she hadn't slept at all that night, but Pippa was snoring happily as usual. It seemed an eternity until morning when she was able to meet her friends in the branches of Mabel, the apple tree. She and Pippa arrived early and Emma waved excitedly as soon as she saw them coming across the field.

'You'll never guess what's happened!' said Emma as they climbed up Mabel. She recounted the saga of the stolen teapot and church roof repair fund.

'Honestly, I knew that Reverend Pritchard could be dim, but this really takes the biscuit!' exclaimed Lizzy.

'Well, if it's any consolation, he was really upset and has learned his lesson for the future,' said Emma.

'Do you think a passing thief took advantage of the unlocked cupboard?' asked Katie.

'I don't think so,' replied Emma. 'That'd be too much of a fluke and Gramps thinks a stranger couldn't have gone into the vestry during the day without being noticed.'

'I guess we should make a list of suspects, taking into consideration those who have access to the vestry and those with motive,' said Katie thoughtfully.

'But how do we assess motive? Do we have to include everyone who's short of money?' asked Laurie.

'That would cover a cast of a thousand!' said Lizzy. 'I'd say it's easier to consider those with access to the vestry.'

'In that case, there's Reverend Pritchard, Miss Prendergast, Mr Smith the organist, and all the bell-ringers,' said Laurie. 'Not Emma's Grandpa or Lizzy's Dad, of course,' she added hastily.

'And Richard and Miss Barnard can't possibly be suspects either,' said Emma.

'Emma, definitely not my Dad and your Grandpa, but real detectives don't just remove suspects from the list because they like them! I very much hope the culprit turns out to be Miss Prendergast because I can't stand her! But that's not how a real detective operates,' said Lizzy.

'You're quite right, of course, Lizzy,' said Emma. 'So, who's going on the list?'

'Okay, we have Reverend Pritchard, Miss Prendergast, Mr Smith, Richard, Miss Barnard, Mr Rogers and Colonel Granger,' said Katie.

'Who else? Who does the flowers and cleans the church?' said Lizzy.

'Good point,' said Emma. 'Well, Granny and Mrs Rogers take it in turns to do the flowers and I think Philip Evans' mum cleans the church.'

'If Philip Evans' mum has access to the church, do you think we should include him as a suspect?' asked Laurie.

'I guess he's a definite possibility,' replied Lizzy.

'I've just had a thought,' said Emma. 'Granny told me that she'd heard a rumour that Mr Rogers' antique business is going under. It looks as though both Mr and Mrs Rogers had motive and access to the church.'

'Yes,' said Lizzy thoughtfully. 'I imagine the delightful Cynthia would do anything to avoid going bankrupt. I'd say they're both strong suspects.'

'Do we know when the teapot was stolen?' asked Katie.

'Reverend Pritchard noticed it had been stolen at eight on Friday 25th July and he thought he'd seen the teapot in the morning or possibly the day before. So, that gives us a fairly tight timeframe. Actually, it's a pity about the teapot too – it was such a lovely shade of turquoise and a really unusual shape. Grandpa told me it's called hexagonal. I always thought it looked like a teapot from *Alice in Wonderland*,' said Emma.

'I guess we should put our thinking caps on, keep our ears open and our eyes peeled,' said Lizzy.

'Yes, and let's take every opportunity to grill the suspects, whenever we meet them!' said Laurie fiercely.

'Agreed,' said one and all.

Chapter Six

The Visit

The next morning, the telephone owl hooted and Granny answered.

'Hilda,' said Granny, 'how lovely to hear from you. How's Alfred?' Granny was silent for a long time while she listened to an account of Alfred and his ailments, merely nodding from time to time, which looked comical as she was nodding to their candlestick telephone!

'Yes, of course, Hilda, it would be lovely to see you. When would you like to come?'

At this, Grandpa put down his newspaper and looked at Granny meaningfully.

'Next Saturday? Yes, of course, that'll be wonderful,' enthused Granny. 'Just let us know the time of your train and Ernest will pick you up from the station. All right then, we look forward to seeing you on Saturday,' and, with that, Granny hung up the telephone.

'Is that what I think it is?' asked Grandpa.

'Hilda's coming to stay, if that's what you mean, Ernest.'

Grandpa gave an involuntary groan and covered his face with his hands.

'Now don't be like that, Ernest. Hilda's my sister and I won't have her denigrated.'

'I'm not denigrating,' said Grandpa indignantly, 'I'm merely groaning!'

'If Hilda's coming on Saturday, that doesn't give us much time to clean the house thoroughly and tidy the garden,' said Granny anxiously. 'Ernest, perhaps you could break… sorry, I mean give the news to the children,' said Granny, looking out of the window and watching Emma, Edward and Pippa merrily engaged in a game of 'Puss, Puss'.

'Yes,' said Grandpa, sighing heavily. 'By the way, did I gather that something's wrong with Alfred? It's strange for Hilda to leave him if he's ill.'

'Well, you know, Alfred. Apparently, he's had one of his turns, but Hilda thinks it will do him good to be alone for a while. Now, don't say anything unkind, Ernest,' said Granny, catching his eye and smiling in spite of herself.

'My lips are sealed,' said Grandpa, going into the garden.

Hilda was Granny's eldest sister but she almost seemed to be from another generation, or possibly from another century. Whereas Granny was fun-loving, Hilda prided herself on moral rectitude, and rooting out foolishness and weakness wherever she found it. Granny was a little awestruck by her own sister, but the rest of her family didn't like Hilda at all.

Grandpa went out into the garden with a heavy heart and interrupted the game. 'Sorry, children but could I have a word with you?'

They trailed into the caravan, looking surprised and then concerned. 'Gramps, what is it?' asked Emma, worriedly. 'Has anything happened to Mum and Dad?'

'No, no, Red,' said Grandpa, reassuringly. 'Don't worry, they're absolutely fine. No, it's nothing like that,' he said hesitantly.

Emma, Edward and Pippa looked at each other in alarm.

'No, it's something nice – it's a visit we should look forward to really. The truth is that Granny's sister, your great-aunt Hilda, is coming to stay on Saturday,' explained Grandpa.

Both children looked appalled and Pippa started to bark. Emma burst out angrily, 'Isn't it enough that Mum and Dad aren't coming to see us? Do we really have to put up with Great-Aunt Hilda instead?'

'Now, Emma, you're being over-dramatic, you know. Hilda's not an ogre and has many good

74

qualities,' Grandpa added, lamely.

'Such as?' said Emma.

'She's well-meaning,' said Grandpa, 'and, at the end of the day, she's your grandmother's sister.'

'But she disapproves of us,' said Edward, looking very small and mutinous.

'If it's any comfort, she disapproves of me, too,' said Grandpa. 'Look children, we must make the best of this, mainly for your grandmother's sake. Granny will be very upset if we don't make her sister welcome, so we must pull together to make her visit as agreeable as possible. Do I make myself clear?'

Two children and one poodle nodded in reluctant agreement.

The following week was taken up with cleaning, tidying and gardening. Everyone at The Syngret felt they had never worked so hard to make the house and garden meet Aunt Hilda's exacting standards.

'Do you think I should wash the curtains?' asked Granny anxiously.

'Oh for goodness' sake, Edith,' said Grandpa in exasperation. 'You're going to be totally exhausted by the time Saturday comes. Anyone would think the Queen was coming to stay.'

'Not at all,' said Granny. 'I just want everything to look its best.'

'Well, I, for one, have had enough. I've done what

I can but I've neglected Myfanwy for ages and I'm now going to spend some time on her.' He stomped into the garden.

'Children,' said Granny, 'why don't you go and play now for a while?'

Emma and Edward immediately looked more cheerful and went into the garden.

'Oh dear, Pippa,' said Granny with a sigh. 'It's such a pity that the prospect of Hilda's visit has made everyone so bad-tempered. I just hope it goes well.' Pippa tried to look sympathetic and wagged her tail gently.

On Saturday morning, Emma made her way, as usual, to Mabel to see her friends.

'Hello, Emma,' said Katie and Laurie as they climbed up into the branches.

'Where's Lizzy?' said Emma in surprise.

'Sorry,' said Laurie. 'I forgot to say that Lizzy's mum said she didn't feel well enough to come this morning.'

'Oh dear,' said Katie, 'has she got a cold or something?'

'I imagine that's what it is,' said Laurie. 'Hopefully, she'll be as right as rain soon.'

'So, can you imagine? I was so looking forward to seeing Mum and Dad and now I get Great-Aunt Hilda instead. It's like having your pet pussy cat snatched away and replaced by a boa constrictor!' declared Emma, dramatically.

'Maybe it won't be so bad,' said Laurie.

'Yes, sometimes when we imagine the worst, things turn out much better,' said Katie.

'Let's hope so,' said Emma. 'Well, here's the promised list of suspects,' she continued, fishing the list out of her bag.

The case of the disappearing teapot (and church roof repair fund)!

The crime: Turquoise teapot, containing £1,000 for the church roof repair fund, was discovered stolen on Friday 25th July at 8pm.
Location: Unlocked cupboard in unlocked church vestry.
Timeframe of crime: Sometime between the morning of Thursday 24th July and 8pm on Friday 25th July.

List of Suspects and their access to the church:

Reverend Pritchard: Access to church at all times.
Miss Prendergast (choir leader): Choir practice was on Wednesday evening, but might she have gone into the church for another choir-related reason?
Mr Smith (church organist): Was he practising the organ during Thursday or Friday?
Farmer Richard Williams: In the church for bell-ringing practice on Friday evening.
Miss Barnard: In the church for bell-ringing practice on Friday evening.

Mr Rogers: In the church for bell-ringing practice on Friday evening. If his antique business is losing money, then he has a strong motive for the theft.

Colonel Granger: In the church for bell-ringing practice on Friday evening.

Mrs Rogers (church flower arranger): Did she arrange flowers on Thursday or Friday? If Mr Rogers' antique business is losing money, then she also has a strong motive for the theft.

Mrs Evans (church cleaner): Did she clean the church on Thursday or Friday?

Philip Evans: already known to be a thief. Might he have come to the church with his mum and seized his chance to steal the teapot?

Are any of the others, apart from Mr and Mrs Rogers, particularly hard up, at present?

'Well,' said Laurie. 'I must say Mr Smith's the most timid man I've ever met – he can hardly look you in the eye when he says, "Good morning." I'd eat my hat if he had the courage to steal anything!'

'But if he was desperate for money, he might've been tempted,' said Katie.

'At least, we've got a clear list of suspects, though,' said Laurie.

'And hopefully we can eliminate them one by one until we are left with the culprit!' exclaimed Emma with relish. 'Anyway, I'd better go back to give Granny a hand. My goodness, how grown-ups fret about things like tidiness!'

Emma made her way back to The Syngret and helped Granny make the final preparations for Hilda's visit.

'Ernest, we need to think about going to the station now, so do come in and change your clothes,' called Granny.

At last, they were ready to leave with Grandpa looking unusually smart in a shirt and jacket.

'Edward!' cried Granny in consternation. 'You've mud on your trousers and jam on your face. You can't possibly go like that.'

'Sorry, I didn't notice,' said Edward.

'Go and change your trousers immediately and wash your face.'

They drove in solemn silence to the station. As usual, they were late so Hilda was already waiting in the station for them, looking grim-faced. Granny jumped out of Major Beetroot, their old red car, and went to greet her. Hilda was even thinner than Granny, with steel grey hair like a helmet, a stern expression and a very upright bearing.

'Hilda, dear,' said Granny, kissing her cheek. 'How lovely to see you. So sorry we're late.'

'Yes,' said Grandpa, approaching with the children. 'Edward managed to get mud on his trousers and had to change them, which held us up.'

Granny frowned at him for admitting this, and Grandpa quickly added, 'How's Alfred? I understand he hasn't been very well.'

'Alfred is prone to dyspepsia, as you know,' said Hilda, 'but he's improving, thank you. I'm glad to see you – I was beginning to think you weren't coming, after all.'

'Yes sorry about that, Hilda,' said Granny, linking her arm through Hilda's and taking her to the car. 'Ernest will bring your suitcase.'

They soon arrived at The Syngret.

'I can't imagine why you keep on such a large house and grounds at your time of life. It's looking as ramshackle as ever,' said Hilda, going in through the front door. At this, Granny looked crestfallen, having spent so long trying to make everything look its best.

'You two, sit down,' said Grandpa, 'and I'll make tea.'

'So, Hilda, how've you been?' asked Granny.

'I am always well, Edith, as you know, and there is always much to occupy my time. So much needs to be done for our charitable deeds centre. Now, let me look at these children,' she said, bringing her critical gaze to bear upon Emma and Edward who, unconsciously, took a step backwards. 'I can see that you have both grown. What have you been doing with yourselves?'

'I've been learning to play the trumpet,' said Edward proudly. 'I'll play a tune for you.' He rushed to find his trumpet and music book. 'Here you are, Aunt Hilda. Choose your favourite piece in this book and I'll play it for you.'

'All right then, if I must,' said Hilda. 'Can you play "There'll Always Be An England"?'

'Um, I must admit I'd be sight-reading that one.'

'I know, Edward,' Grandpa interjected quickly, 'let's have "We'll Meet Again". I think that's your very best.'

Edward launched into the tune, but as he was nervous he didn't do it, or himself, justice. There was an embarrassed silence at the end, after which Hilda said, 'Edith, why did you choose such a very loud instrument for Edward?'

'Actually,' said Grandpa, 'it was my choice, as I found a very good quality trumpet in a second-hand shop.' He quickly left the room before he could say anything rude.

'And what about you, Emma?' said Hilda.

'School only finished last week,' said Emma.

'Emma did exceptionally well in her exams,' said Granny.

'And the choir came top in the choral competition,' added Emma.

'Good, but have you been helping your grandmother and making yourself useful?' asked Hilda.

'Yes, I think so,' said Emma, looking perplexed.

'And I've been helping Gramps with Myfanwy,' added Edward.

'Who is Myfanwy?' asked Hilda in surprise.

'She's a boat,' explained Edward. 'Come outside and I'll show you.'

Hilda followed Edward outside and beheld the duck-blue egg dinghy with the mermaid at its prow. 'Gramps has worked really hard on her,' said Edward. 'Her engine didn't work at all at the start and Gramps has spent hours on getting her going.'

'How extraordinary,' remarked Hilda.

'Yes,' said Edward quietly, realising that Great-Aunt Hilda did not seem as impressed as he was. 'Shall we go back inside now then?' he added uncertainly.

'Yes, indeed,' said Hilda in a grim tone.

Back in the living room, Emma was having a game of chase with Pippa who was barking gaily. They stopped as soon as Hilda came back into the room.

'I always think that poodles are the most irritating of dogs and what ridiculous fur they have!' exclaimed Hilda.

'Pippa is the best of all dogs with the most beautiful fur!' said Emma, heatedly. Granny shot her a warning glance.

At that moment, Hilda gave a loud shriek.

'Hilda, what is it?' asked Granny in concern.

'A white mouse has just popped out of Edward's pocket,' said Hilda, backing away from Edward. 'I can't stand mice.'

'Oh, that's only Louis Armstrong,' explained Edward. 'He's not really a mouse – he's my friend.'

'How extraordinary,' exclaimed Hilda. 'Edith, are you *really* happy for Edward to keep vermin?'

'Well, Ed had his heart set on a mouse and it does seem very harsh to call Louis Armstrong vermin,' said Granny.

'Louis Armstrong is *not* vermin!' shouted Edward with tears in his eyes and he ran from the room.

Granny and Emma looked at each other.

Minutes later, Emma and Pippa went into the kitchen, where they found Grandpa and Edward munching their toast and looking glum.

'How long did Aunt Hilda say she'd be here?' whispered Emma.

'She didn't,' said Grandpa, and Pippa raised her eyes heavenwards.

The next day, the cuckoo sounded at 10am, just as everyone was clearing up the breakfast things. 'What on earth was that?' said Hilda. 'It sounded just like a cuckoo.'

'Ah, you see how witty and original Ernest is with his contraptions. Instead of a doorbell, we have the sound of a cuckoo,' said Granny.

'How extraordinary,' said Hilda.

'I think it's rather wonderful,' said Granny defensively. 'Do you remember how we used to go to Portmeirion as children, Hilda, and it was full of surprising, witty touches? I always think that the architect must have been a bit like my Ernest.' She smiled her sweet smile.

In the meanwhile, Emma had gone to open the door and found Katie and Laurie looking anxious on the doorstep.

'It's so great to see you,' said Emma. 'Granny, Katie and Laurie are here and I'm just taking them to the swings,' she called.

'But it's only ten,' said Hilda. 'In my day, I would never have entertained visitors until my household chores were done.'

Emma shut the front door more loudly than was polite.

'She's insufferable,' fumed Emma, 'even worse than I remember. I wondered how long it would be before she started to say, "In my day". I can't believe she's a close relation of Granny, who's such fun. I suppose there's absolutely no chance Great-Aunt Hilda could be our arch-criminal? Then Constable Roberts could forcibly remove her!'

They walked to the four old swings at the far end of the garden. They were no longer swings but more like moving seats. They each took one of them.

'I'm afraid we've very worrying news,' said Katie.

'Yes,' said Laurie. 'We called in to see if Lizzy was better and it turns out she has scarlet fever.'

'Like Beth in *Little Women*?' asked Katie, and promptly burst into tears.

'Oh no,' said Emma in dismay, 'but children don't get scarlet fever anymore, do they?'

'Unfortunately, it seems they do,' said Laurie quietly.

'So, how ill is she?' asked Emma in alarm.

'Lizzy's mum wouldn't let us see her,' said Laurie. 'Apparently, she's in bed and has started taking antibiotics.'

'But she isn't in hospital then, or anything?' said Emma in relief.

'No, not yet,' said tender-hearted Katie.

'Yes, you may remember that Beth recovers from the scarlet fever in *Little Women*, but is never the same again, and in *Good Wives* she just goes downhill and dies,' said Laurie in a wobbly tone of voice. At that, they burst into violent sobs.

'I know,' said Emma suddenly. 'Let's go to St Mary Magdalene and light a candle for Lizzy's recovery.'

Katie and Laurie nodded in agreement and they headed down to the church. They solemnly lit a candle each in front of the rose window.

'Please, God,' pleaded Laurie, 'let Lizzy recover.'

'And be strong and healthy again,' said Emma.

'And not die like Beth in *Little Women*,' added Katie.

Leaving the church, Laurie said, 'Let's meet up here at eleven tomorrow and go to Lizzy's house for the latest news.'

'Good idea,' agreed the others.

The next morning, Emma and Pippa slipped out of The Syngret as quietly as possible in the hope of not being noticed by Great-Aunt Hilda. Emma picked a bunch of red and cream roses from the garden and then made her way to the church. She waved when she saw Katie and Laurie.

'Oh, what lovely flowers,' said Katie, her pink and white face lighting up.

'Look, Katie and I bought this box of milk chocolates in the hope that Lizzy will soon feel up to eating them,' said Laurie.

'So, shall we go then?' asked Katie. 'Let's hope our prayers have been answered.'

So, three worried girls and one subdued poodle walked solemnly past the Splash and across the village. Lizzy's house was at the end of the village in one of the charming former alms houses, with a beautiful garden at the front, full of hollyhocks, honeysuckle and climbing roses. They knocked the old-fashioned knocker and Lizzy's glamorous, red-haired mother opened the door.

'Hello, Mrs Jones. We were wondering how Lizzy is?' said Laurie tentatively.

'I'm delighted to say she's much better,' said Mrs Jones. 'Would you like to see her?'

'Oh yes, please,' they replied.

They went in and climbed the narrow staircase to Lizzy's room. Lizzy was still in bed, but sitting up. She was wearing her purple pyjamas, with her long straight brown hair in a plait down her back, and looking much as usual.

'I'm so glad to see you,' she said. They sat on the bed and Pippa jumped up and licked her on the nose.

'How are you, Lizzy?' asked Emma.

'Fine really, now that the antibiotics are working. Mum said I was delirious a couple of days ago, but I can't remember much,' said Lizzy.

'We've been so worried about you, Lizzy,' said Katie, her blue eyes filling up with tears. Pippa licked Katie's nose.

'Did you imagine I was going to die like Beth in *Little Women*?' said Lizzy.

'How did you guess?' gasped Laurie.

'Really though,' said Emma, 'if only Beth and others like her had been able to take antibiotics, none of them would have died. Thank heavens we're not living in the nineteenth century.'

'I almost forgot,' said Laurie, 'here's a box of

chocolates for you.'

'And here are some roses,' said Emma.

'Thank you very much everyone,' said Lizzy, looking touched. 'It's so kind of you. Well, I've been dying to hear – how are you getting on with solving our mystery?'

'As you can imagine, not so well without our very own Sherlock Holmes!' exclaimed Katie with a smile.

'I managed to find out from my mum,' said Laurie, 'that the church is cleaned on a Saturday and that's when choir practice takes place.'

'I know this isn't hard evidence,' mused Lizzy, 'but I find it hard to believe that Father Pritchard would have stolen his own teapot when the whole episode makes him look so stupid!'

'That pretty much narrows it down to the bell-ringers then, doesn't it?' said Emma thoughtfully.

'Yes, I'd say they're our prime suspects, with possibly Mr and Mrs Rogers in the lead,' said Laurie.

'Okay, girls,' said Lizzy's Mum, popping her head round the door. 'Lizzy's still recovering, you know, so she'd better have a rest now.'

'Oh dear,' said Emma, rolling her eyes. 'That means I'll have to get back to Great-Aunt Hilda and do some chores.'

'See you again soon then, my dear, dear friends,' said Lizzy.

'Take care of yourself. See you at Mabel's on

Saturday,' said Emma and three happy voices said, 'Agreed.'

Back at The Syngret, things were not going smoothly.

'Why on earth do you have a greenhouse covered in old clothes?' asked Hilda, disapprovingly.

'Actually,' said Grandpa, 'we couldn't afford to replace the glass or the entire greenhouse for that matter, and then we discovered that it works just as well by covering the broken panes in old clothes.'

'But it looks ridiculous and people will think you are mad,' said Hilda.

'Let them,' said Grandpa, biting his lip and he went out to work on Myfanwy.

'Have you tasted the tomatoes, though, Hilda?' asked Granny. 'They're the most delicious tomatoes any of us have ever eaten. I think they taste much better than they did when the greenhouse actually had glass in it!'

'I just don't understand why you and Ernest can't behave normally.'

'Don't you think, Hilda, that it's best to live and let live?' said Granny gently. 'After all, Ernest and I aren't hurting anyone.'

'Well, you are my sister and, of course, I am very fond of you, but I can't pretend to understand your bohemian existence.'

At this, Granny laughed merrily. 'Honestly, Hilda,

anyone would think we were nudists living in a commune, to hear you talk.'

'Anyway, as I have been away for nearly a week, I think I ought to go home and see how Alfred is. It has been very nice to see you nevertheless, Edith, and thank you for having me to stay,' said Hilda gruffly.

'You know you'll always be welcome.'

At that moment, Grandpa popped his head around the kitchen door.

'I know that Emma went to see Lizzy, but have either of you seen Edward?'

'Not since breakfast,' said Hilda.

'He's probably outside playing,' said Granny.

Grandpa went around the garden looking for Edward without success. He was beginning to worry but, when passing the caravan, he heard sobbing.

'Edward, is that you?' Grandpa went into the caravan and saw a small figure huddled on the bed. 'What on earth's the matter?' said Grandpa in concern, going over to the bed and sitting down.

'Oh, Gramps, it's terrible.' Edward was so distressed that he was clutching Llewellyn, the strange, elongated, knitted old teddy bear which had belonged to his mother as a child. Louis Armstrong was sitting on Edward's shirt, looking up at him with concern.

'What is it, my darling boy? Please tell me at once.'

'I wanted to surprise you by getting into the brass

band. So I secretly arranged an audition with Miss Prendergast. Oh, Gramps, she said I was no good at the trumpet.' With that, he cried harder than ever.

'Oh dear, Ed,' said Grandpa in dismay. 'Please tell me, exactly what did she say?'

It was a while before Edward could control his hiccoughing sobs in order to respond. 'I played "We'll Meet Again" because you said it was my best. Miss Prendergast said I had no technique, was a very poor standard even for a beginner, and could not read music well enough. She said she doubted I'd ever be able to join the brass band.'

'Edward *bach*, I'm very sorry you have had this setback, but the world's full of great musicians who have suffered such blows from unimaginative and uncaring so-called professionals.'

'Really, Gramps?' said Edward, looking a little less upset.

'Yes, really. Now, I tell you what – dry your eyes and let's go for a walk along the beach. I'll buy you a ninety-nine ice cream.'

'Yes, Gramps. I'll try to cheer up.'

'That's my boy,' said Grandpa, and that's what they did. It was a beautiful evening and they admired the flaming sunset over the sea. On their return, Granny was busy making scrambled eggs and toast, and Emma was laying the table.

'You may be relieved to hear that I am going home

tomorrow morning,' said Hilda. 'I really need to get back to the charitable deeds centre – and to Alfred, of course. But it has been very nice to see you and thank you for having me to stay.'

They were so delighted that Aunt Hilda was going home that they became exceptionally nice to her all of a sudden.

'Hilda,' said Grandpa, 'are you sure you need to go back so soon? You're very welcome to stay, you know.' Granny looked at him in amazement.

'That's very kind, but I really must go.'

'Shall we play a game, as this is your last evening?' said Emma.

'What about battleaxes?' said Edward.

'I think you mean *Battleships*,' said Grandpa, trying to hide a smile.

'I like *Scrabble*,' said Hilda. 'As it's, at least, educational.' They had a game with Emma playing alongside Edward to help him.

By midnight, everyone was sleeping and Pippa was, as usual, snoring gently on Emma's bed. Until there was an almighty shriek coming from Hilda's room. Emma sprang up and went to see what was happening. She met Granny and Gramps on the landing outside Hilda's room. Hilda gave yet another loud shriek.

'Hilda, dear, what is it?' called Granny through

the door. 'Are you ill?'

'Hilda, we're coming in now,' said Grandpa firmly.

By this time, Edward had also emerged to see what was happening. They all went into Hilda's room to see her standing on a chair looking very shaken. Emma and Edward had to make a real effort not to laugh as Hilda was wearing an immense pink hairnet over her helmet hair.

'Look,' said Hilda, pointing at the bed. 'That mouse is in my bed!'

Everyone turned to look at the bed and beheld Louis Armstrong looking very comfortable on Aunt Hilda's pillow.

'Edward,' said Gramps. 'How did Louis Armstrong get in here?'

Edward put on his most innocent expression and said, 'I have no idea, Gramps.'

'Take him away at once,' said Gramps sternly and Edward did as he was told.

Granny and Gramps helped Hilda down from the chair and changed the pillowcase for her.

'Well, I doubt I'll be able to sleep another wink now,' said Hilda. 'Thank goodness this is my last night here.'

Gramps bit his lip in order not to voice agreement with this sentiment!

In the morning, everyone was feeling better and

Edward kept Louis Armstrong hidden away. The children kissed Aunt Hilda on each cheek which pleased her, and she even deigned to stroke Pippa's head in farewell. Granny gave her a big hug.

'Take care of yourself, Hilda, dear, give our love to Alfred and tell him we hope to see him soon.'

'Goodbye, goodbye,' said the children, waving, as Major Beetroot started up at last.

'Well, children,' said Granny. 'I think that went off very well in the end, despite Louis Armstrong. But I'm so exhausted I must go and lie down,' she said, yawning.

'Gosh, I hope things can get back to normal now,' said Emma.

'Yes,' said Edward, looking glum.

'What's the matter, Edward?' said Emma, looking surprised. 'I know – why don't you go and practise your trumpet in the caravan?'

'No thanks,' said Edward, his big, blue eyes filling with tears, and he left the room.

At that moment, Grandpa returned, looking remarkably cheerful and humming 'Doo dah day!'

'What's up with Ed?' asked Emma.

'I'm afraid he's had a trumpeting disappointment. He auditioned for the brass band and was given a resounding rejection by the dreaded Miss Prendergast.'

'Oh dear, poor Ed. Miss Prendergast's not exactly

the easiest person in the world, I know.'

'You can say that again,' muttered Grandpa. 'By the way, where's your grandmother?'

'She's gone to lie down.'

Grandpa went to find Granny, who was lying down with cucumber slices over her eyes.

'What on earth are you doing, Edie?' asked Grandpa.

'What does it look like? I'm exhausted after all the cleaning and entertaining and I am resting. Cucumber's supposed to be soothing and restorative for the eyes.'

'Well, can I just talk to you about Ed's great upset?'

Granny removed the cucumber slices and sat up. 'What's Ed's great upset?' she said in alarm.

'Yesterday he auditioned for the brass band, and Miss Prendergast told him he's hopeless at the trumpet.'

'Oh dear, dear.'

'I really have a mind to tell that woman what I think of her,' said Grandpa heatedly.

'Aren't music teachers supposed to encourage children in their love of music rather than destroying their hopes and dreams? It's almost incredible.'

'Yes I know, Ernest, but please don't say anything to Miss Prendergast. She's also Emma's music teacher and we don't want to cause any unpleasantness for Emma, especially when she's so upset her parents aren't visiting this summer.'

'But what shall we do, then?'

'I'm afraid, Ernest, that it's partly our fault,' said Granny with a sigh.

'What do you mean?' said Grandpa in astonishment.

'I never thought I'd say this. Ed has shown a lot of determination and dedication to the trumpet. However, without proper lessons, how can he make progress or learn proper trumpet technique?'

'Yes, I see,' said Grandpa thoughtfully. 'He ought to have lessons.'

'I tell you what, let's make enquiries about a good trumpet teacher.'

'Unfortunately, we can't afford it, Edie,' said Grandpa, ruefully shaking his head.

'I'm sure Mark and Sarah will pay for lessons. After all, Emma has singing and piano lessons.'

'Of course, I might have guessed you'd come up with the perfect solution.'

'Yes, Ernest. And now, if you don't mind, I'll get back to my siesta and my cucumber slices!' said Granny.

Chapter Seven

The Birthday Party

Emma's birthday was coming soon. Grandpa and Granny were determined that she should have an enjoyable time, partly in the hope that it would make up for the disappointment of not seeing her parents over the summer, and also for having to endure Aunt Hilda's visit.

Shortly after Aunt Hilda's departure, Granny and Grandpa sat Emma down, and Grandpa said, 'My darling girl, we'd love you to have your heart's desire on your birthday...'

'In as far as we are able to offer it,' added Granny hastily.

'So, what would you like for your birthday?' asked Grandpa. 'Your grandmother and I thought we could go on a picnic in Snowdonia, or what about a boat trip to the Isle of Man?'

'Or shall we go to see *Twelfth Night* at the Grand

Theatre in Llandudno? What do you think, my darling?' asked Granny.

'Granny and Gramps, it's extremely kind of you to give my birthday so much thought. All those ideas sound great, but do you know what I'd really like?' asked Emma.

They both looked at her expectantly.

'Please could I invite Lizzy, Laurie and Katie to a formal birthday lunch party which I'd cook and serve myself? You and Gramps could go out for the day, and if Edward and Pippa would help me as waiters, that's what I'd really like.'

'What a great idea!' exclaimed Grandpa.

'Well, it sounds a good idea in principle,' said Granny doubtfully 'but, as you know, I only ever open a tin, or make eggs and toast.'

'Yes, but if I'm ever to be the hostess with the mostest, I'll have to start learning soon,' said Emma brightly. 'Anyway, how hard can it be to follow a recipe?'

At this, Pippa looked at her quizzically.

'If you're really sure, my dear girl,' said Granny. 'We will, of course, help you as much as we can.'

'Splendid,' said Grandpa. 'I'll get out the cookery books and you can choose a menu. We'll draw up the shopping list, then Major Beetroot and I will drive you into Colwyn.'

So, over the next few days, Emma and Pippa

pored over recipes and finally decided on a menu for the momentous occasion. Emma wrote the invitations to Lizzy, Laurie and Katie:

Miss Emma Thomas
requests the pleasure of the company of
Miss Katie Edwards/Miss Lizzy Jones/Miss Laurie
Price
at her birthday luncheon
on
Saturday 21st August at 12.30pm.

The menu will include:
Stuffed king prawns
Steak à la Syngret
Trifle Pompadour
All accompanied by lemonade grand cru!

Please bring a party trick!

At this, Grandpa smiled and Granny bit her lip. The girls swiftly accepted the invitation and, a few days before the great event, Emma went with Grandpa and Major Beetroot to Colwyn, with her precious shopping list clasped tightly in her hand, and looking very serious at the great responsibility resting on her shoulders.

The day of Emma's birthday dawned soon.

Emma got up early to lay the dining room table with Granny's best cutlery and crockery. She also put vases of fresh red and white roses from the garden around the room, and on the piano, with candles placed strategically for best effect.

'How lovely the old room looks!' exclaimed Granny.

'Okay, Red, your grandmother and I will be off to Colwyn for the day then,' said Grandpa, as they climbed into Major Beetroot. 'Goodbye and good luck.'

'Have a wonderful time, Granny and Gramps,' cried the children as Major Beetroot's engine finally sprang into action.

As the car disappeared from view, Emma, Edward and Pippa looked at each other, none of them daring to admit how daunted they felt at the prospect ahead.

'Let's get cracking!' said Emma in her jolliest tone. 'Ed, please can you put ice in the lemonade, and bread in the basket?'

All three rushed around, but not much actual cooking was done. Shortly afterwards, the cuckoo sounded.

'Blast, the guests have already arrived,' said Edward, looking worried.

'Oh my goodness!' exclaimed Emma. 'How can it be twelve-thirty already? Edward, please can you show them into the living room?'

'Okay, keep your apron on,' said Edward.

Lizzy, Laurie and Katie went into the living room, chatting merrily.

'I think you ought to go in to say hello,' said Edward. 'They're your guests, after all.'

Emma joined them in the living room still wearing her apron, her face flushed and carrying her homemade, iced lemonade.

'Hello, everyone,' she said. 'Thanks so much for coming.'

'Happy birthday to you,' they sang, giving her a kiss. 'Here are your cards and presents.'

'Thanks,' said Emma. 'If you don't mind, I won't open them just now. I'm afraid lunch isn't ready yet. Just talk amongst yourselves and have a glass of lemonade.'

'Great, sounds like a good idea,' said Lizzy diplomatically. She poured each of the girls a glass, but they flinched as they drank it. The drink was quite bitter, and they set down their glasses quickly.

At that moment, the cuckoo sounded once again.

Who on earth can that be? thought Emma crossly. *Everyone's already arrived.*

It then occurred to her that perhaps Granny and Grandpa had decided to return after all, and she dashed to the door in happy relief, only to find Mrs

Rogers standing on the doorstep.

'Oh, Mrs Rogers!' exclaimed Emma, looking appalled.

'Hello, dear,' said Mrs Rogers. 'I was just passing and I thought I'd catch up with your grandmother. I need to speak to her about the flower rota for the church.'

'I'm very sorry,' said Emma, 'but Granny and Grandpa have gone to Colwyn for the day. I don't expect them back for ages.'

'Aren't you going to invite me in?' said Mrs Rogers.

'Well, actually, I'm just having a lunch party for my friends. It's my birthday, you see,' said Emma.

'How kind of you to include me,' said Mrs Rogers, walking into the house 'and many happy returns, dear!'

Emma felt horrified, but was helpless to stop Mrs Rogers at full tilt. In fact, she could not think of another word to say. She meekly followed Mrs Rogers into the living room. Lizzy, Laurie and Katie were chatting gaily, but they fell silent at the sight of Mrs Rogers.

'Hello, Mrs Rogers,' said Katie, lamely.

'Hello, Katie dear,' said Mrs Rogers. 'Emma has kindly invited me to join you for lunch while I wait for her grandmother to return.' Under different circumstances, Emma might have felt amused to see how miserable her friends looked at Mrs Rogers' unwelcome arrival, and she was amazed that even someone as insensitive as Mrs Rogers did not notice.

'Mrs Rogers,' said Lizzy, seizing the opportunity to do some detective work. 'What do you make of the stolen teapot and the theft of the church roof fund?'

'Shocking, absolutely shocking,' declared Mrs Rogers.

'What do you think could have happened?' asked Katie, opening her eyes innocently.

'I find it difficult to believe that it could be anyone we know,' mused Mrs Rogers. 'I expect it was someone just passing through. They must have sneaked into the church to see what could be stolen. There's a lot of riff-raff around nowadays.'

None of the girls could think of anything in reply, and an awkward silence fell.

Meanwhile, Emma went into the kitchen and stared in concern at the king prawns. After a while, Laurie dashed into the kitchen, flicking her dark hair out of her eyes.

'Is there a problem?' she said in a stage whisper.

'Oh, Laurie, I had no idea these prawns would take forever to thaw.'

'Goodness, they do still seem to be frozen, don't they? Can you put them under cold running water?' asked Laurie.

'That's a good idea. Thanks,' said Emma.

'What are you going to stuff them with?' asked Laurie practically.

'To be honest, I gave up on the stuffing idea. I've just got a sauce with garlic and lemon in that pan over there,' said Emma.

'As soon as these prawns thaw out, we can fry them,' said Laurie, pummelling the prawns with her large fist. 'But Emma, it's excruciating in there. We've already run out of topics of conversation with Mrs Rogers and, frankly, none of us had anything to say to her in the first place.'

'Can't you interview her. You might be able to work out if she or Mr Rogers has stolen the vicar's teapot?' said Emma. 'She might let slip some information about their financial situation.'

'Lizzy did try, but asking personal questions is easier said than done,' said Laurie, doubtfully.

'Then, you'll have to entertain her for a while,' said Emma.

At that moment, Edward came into the kitchen. 'What the hell's going on?' he said.

'Edward, don't swear,' said Emma automatically.

'If ever there was a day for swearing,' complained Edward. 'This is it.'

'Edward, can you amuse them while I fry the prawns?' asked Emma. 'Play your trumpet or something.'

'I can't. I haven't been practising,' grumbled Edward.

'Please, dear Edward,' urged Laurie.

'Fair enough,' agreed a reluctant Edward, and he went off to find his trumpet.

'Okay, everyone, we're going to have some pre-lunch entertainment,' announced Laurie, loudly banging the old gong in the living room. 'I present Master Edward Thomas on trumpet,' and, taking their cue, Lizzy and Katie started to applaud in encouragement.

'What're you playing, Edward?' whispered Laurie.

'Oh yes,' said Edward. 'This is the Toreador's song from the opera, *Carmen*.'

He launched into it with enthusiasm, but the choice was over-ambitious. Lizzy, Laurie and Katie clapped along, partly to pretend they were enjoying it, and partly to keep Edward in time with the music. A look of disbelief flitted across Mrs Rogers' face. As the music finished, the girls applauded tumultuously.

'I must say, Edward. I had no idea you played the trumpet,' said Mrs Rogers.

'Yes,' said Lizzy. 'He's come on in leaps and bounds.'

'He really wasn't very good a few months ago. Nothing compared to now,' said Laurie earnestly.

At this, Katie was overcome with laughter, and had to pretend to cough instead. She ended up having to swallow the bitter lemonade, which made her cough in earnest.

'What on earth do we do now?' Lizzy whispered to Laurie, looking despairing.

'Edward,' said Laurie half-heartedly. 'Can you do anything else?'

Edward thought for a moment. 'I know,' he said. He rushed off and came back wearing a sequinned bolero jacket, false moustache from the dressing-up box, and red scarf with bells and tassels on it. He was accompanied by Pippa, who was sporting a sequinned bow around her neck.

He whispered in Laurie's ear for a moment and she jumped up, exclaiming in a faux Spanish accent, 'Staying with the theme of the Toreador, Ladies and Gentlemen, *Mesdames et Messieurs, damas y caballeros,* I give you Enrico, the famous bull-fighter from Granada,' she said. 'And this is the most dangerous bull in Spain,' she added, pointing at Pippa. The duo then threw themselves with gusto into their bull-fighting routine, where Edward held up the red scarf and Pippa ran into it ferociously. Lizzy, Katie and Laurie desperately tried to make the most of the situation by clapping along and shouting '*Olé*' from time to time, and Katie even took one of the red roses and held it between her teeth.

'Good heavens, children,' said Mrs Rogers. 'What talent you have nowadays!'

'I know,' said Laurie. 'I'll check on the prawns.' She dashed into the kitchen. 'Please, Emma, I beg you... whatever the prawns are like, frozen, raw, still alive, rotten to the core, please put us out of our misery and dish them up!'

'As it happens, I think everything's ready now, so please sound the gong again and luncheon can begin!' said Emma.

They moved into the dining room, and exclaimed with pleasure at the flowers and candles.

'There's been a slight change to the menu,' said Emma. 'We now have king prawns *au citron*!' she said, brandishing a large platter of prawns. 'Do help yourself to lemonade, Mrs Rogers,' she added. 'And you'd better have my place at the table. I need to cook the rest of it while you're eating the prawns.'

'I'll give you a hand in the kitchen,' said Lizzy. 'Oh dear, what's that burning smell?' she said in consternation as they entered the kitchen.

'Oh no, it's the potatoes!' cried Emma. She looked at the pan sorrowfully. 'Lizzy, do you think any of them can be rescued?'

'Probably not,' said Lizzy sadly, looking at the burnt pan. 'But never mind, there's lots of lovely French bread.'

'Yes,' said Emma cheering up, while heating the

oil in the frying pan, 'and I can't go wrong with cooking steak, can I?'

Shortly afterwards, Edward came into the kitchen.

'Ah, Edward,' said Emma, 'you're just in time to take the steak through to the dining room and, if I say so myself, it does look very good.'

Edward picked up the platter and walked out of the kitchen. There was a sudden, spectacular clatter of crockery, a great hullabaloo of exclamation and a shrieking and barking of poodle. Emma dashed into the dining room. 'What on earth's happened? Are you okay?' she said.

Edward and the steaks were lying on the carpet. 'I'm so sorry, Emma,' said Edward plaintively. 'I tripped over Pippa coming into the room!'

'Edward, how could you be so clumsy?' cried Emma. 'Perhaps we can rescue the steaks? I'm sure this carpet's clean. What do you think?'

Lizzy said quietly, 'I'm afraid that Pippa has already tasted several of them, Emma.'

'Pippa, how could you?' said Emma. 'This really is the last straw,' and she promptly burst into tears.

'Never mind, Emma,' said Laurie. 'I couldn't help noticing you have cheese and salad in the fridge and, together with the French bread, they'll make a lovely lunch.'

'Oh goodness me, is that the time?' exclaimed

Mrs Rogers in her most phoney manner. 'I promised to meet my husband, Roger, in Colwyn at three o'clock. I'd better get going, but thank you very much for having me and it was lovely to see you again.'

'I thought you wanted to see Granny,' said Emma.

'I do, but it will have to wait for another day,' said Mrs Rogers, collecting her handbag and heading for the door. 'It's been a most memorable afternoon!' She gave them a pseudo royal wave as she left.

They tucked into cheese salad and tried to make the best of the meal for Emma's sake, but she could not be comforted.

'Isn't that woman awful?' said Edward.

'Yes, and can you believe she has a husband called Roger Rogers?' said Katie.

'Only she could manage that,' said Lizzy.

'Did you see her face when she tasted the lemonade?' said Laurie.

'Do you mean there's something wrong with it?' said Emma.

'To be honest, it didn't have nearly enough sugar,' said Lizzy apologetically.

'I don't believe you,' said Emma heatedly. 'I think you're just being horrible now.' She had a taste and then said, 'Oh, my goodness. It's the most bitter lemonade ever!' She burst into tears.

Emma's friends and Edward looked at each other and one by one started to chuckle. The more they looked at each other, the more they laughed, until they were laughing uncontrollably with tears streaming down their faces.

'Stop it!' cried Emma. 'How can you mock me on this worst of all possible birthdays? It's so unfair. It's all your fault, Edward. If you hadn't dropped the steak, we might have carried it off. Even Pippa let me down.'

'Well,' said Edward heatedly. 'You're the most ungrateful sister in the whole of Wales, as well as the bossiest! I've been ordered around all day. I played my trumpet for that horrible woman, and Pippa and I even performed our bull-fighting act. I don't ask for thanks, but I don't expect to be blamed for your cooking disasters.' With that, he flounced out of the room.

At this, Emma cried more and everyone else laughed harder but, for the sake of Emma's feelings, they tried not to.

'Oh, go away and leave me!' cried Emma melodramatically and she ran upstairs to her bedroom. The three girls looked at each other shamefacedly and then burst out laughing again.

Later, they crept up to Emma's room which was locked.

'Emma,' said Lizzy. 'We're going now.'

'We're sorry you're so miserable,' said Laurie, 'but hope you'll see the funny side of this later.'

'Yes, it does seem a pity to be so upset on your birthday,' said Katie.

Granny and Grandpa returned shortly afterwards to find the kitchen and dining room in a mess, and no sign of Emma, Edward or Pippa. In alarm, Granny went upstairs and tried to open the door of Emma's bedroom. She felt even more alarmed to find it locked.

'Emma, it's Granny!' she called. 'Please let me in.' Emma unlocked and opened the door. Her face was wet, and her eyes were all scrunched up and red. She blew her nose and said, 'Oh, Granny, I should have listened to you. The whole thing was an absolute disaster. I am the hostess with the leastest!' and she recounted the events of the whole sorry day, including the visit of Mrs Rogers.

When she had finished, Granny looked at her and said, 'I'm very sorry indeed that your birthday didn't go according to plan, but you must admit it's very funny.' With that, she started to laugh. Emma looked at her and slowly she began to laugh too. She laughed until the tears rolled down her cheeks.

'And you should have seen Mrs Rogers' face when Edward played the trumpet, and then went into his bull-fighting routine with Pippa. She must've thought she was in a mad house when the steak landed on the carpet. Pippa knows that I'm angry with her and I haven't seen her since. Oh dear, do you think my friends are still talking to me?' She went downstairs and opened her cards and presents. Her favourite present was Lizzy's, which was a pencil case in the shape of a black poodle! She helped Granny and Grandpa to clear up the mess and then went to find Edward who was sulking in the caravan with Pippa.

'Edward, Pippa, are you in there?' said Emma tentatively.

'Go away,' said Edward. 'We don't want to talk to you.'

'Don't be like that, Ed,' said Emma. 'I'm truly sorry that I blamed you for everything when you only tried to help me, really I am.'

'Oh, all right then,' said Edward with a sigh, letting Emma into the caravan.

'And I guess it was too great a temptation for Pippa to see several freshly cooked steaks on the carpet,' said Emma, stroking Pippa's curly black head.

'You must admit, Emma, that this is probably the funniest birthday you're ever likely to have,' said Edward, giggling.

'Yes, and one of the most memorable.' All three of them, including Pippa, laughed once more.

*

As it was the summer holidays, the girls were due to meet up at Mabel's the following day.

'Thank you so much for the wonderful cards and presents,' said Emma. 'Can you ever forgive me for being such a miserable spoilsport?'

They all started talking at once.

'Don't be silly,' said Katie.

'To be honest, Emma, it was one of the funniest days of my life,' said Laurie.

'Yes, I don't think any of us will ever forget your birthday,' said Lizzy.

'All the same, I think cookery is not my number one talent,' said Emma.

'Luckily,' said Lizzy. 'You have plenty of others!'

'By the way,' said Emma. 'What happened when you tried to cross-examine Mrs Rogers?'

'Well, we didn't get very far,' said Laurie.

'She certainly didn't look guilty and was adamant that the thief must be someone passing through the village,' said Katie.

'Of course, even if she was the teapot thief, she would say that, wouldn't she?' said Lizzy. 'So, sadly, we're no further forward.'

Chapter Eight

All At Sea

The next time they all met up was a perfect summer's day. It was warm and sunny, with a light breeze, and small white clouds scudding across a bright blue sky. Emma, Lizzy, Laurie and Katie had arranged to spend the day at the seaside. The tourists congregated on the main beach, but the locals knew a much more beautiful area called 'Splashford Sands'. This they considered to be their own personal territory. They walked along in flip-flops, carrying all their beach paraphernalia with them. Pippa pranced along with her ball in her mouth. Everyone anticipated a magical day ahead. As soon as they got onto the sand, they took off their sundresses as their swimsuits were underneath. Emma breathed in the salty air from the sea and the delicious aroma of wet sand. These were her favourite smells of all.

'Well,' said Emma, 'do any of you have anything

to report on the "Case of the Missing Teapot"?'

'Nothing whatsoever from my end,' said Lizzy mournfully.

'Me neither,' said Laurie.

'Oh, it's such a lovely day, can't we just forget about the dratted teapot for today?' said Katie.

'Let's make the best sandcastle ever,' said Emma, 'with turrets and a huge moat.'

They worked together, with Laurie and Lizzy constructing the towers and turrets, Emma digging the surrounding moat, and little Katie dashing back and forth with buckets of water to fill it. When it was finished, they stopped to admire their masterpiece.

'My goodness, our castle's even better than the one in *Sleeping Beauty*!' exclaimed Lizzy.

'Such a pity that the tide will destroy our work of art when it comes in,' said Laurie. The tide was far out, leaving several rock pools, including one large, deep one.

'Look, I can see an anemone in the pool,' said Lizzy.

'But I hate crabs,' said Katie, shuddering. 'Something about the way they scuttle about is really creepy.'

'I've found the most gorgeous stone!' exclaimed Lizzy, holding it aloft. She suddenly screamed and dropped it, and Laurie and Emma rushed over to her.

'Lizzy, what's the matter?' asked Emma.

'After I picked it up,' said Lizzy, 'I realised it was a jelly fish.'

'At least, if it's on the beach, it's dead and can't sting you,' said Laurie sensibly.

'Does anyone fancy a game of badminton?' suggested Lizzy.

'Yes, I do,' said Laurie.

'Emma, please can you help me inflate the lilo?' asked Katie.

'Of course,' agreed Emma, 'but you mustn't take it on the sea, Katie, just on the rock pool.' When they'd finished, Emma said, 'Pippa's been waiting patiently for a game, so I'll throw the ball for her now.' She smiled as Pippa raced across the sand. 'Pip's so sweet and easy to please,' said Emma fondly to herself.

At that moment, they heard the chug of a dinghy's engine and turned to see Grandpa and Myfanwy proudly crossing the bay.

'Hello, Gramps and Myfanwy, how lovely to see you!' called Emma, waving.

'Isn't it a beautiful day,' said Grandpa. 'Are you having a good time?'

'Great, thanks,' they called back.

Grandpa had never been seen in swimming trunks (and secretly vowed that he never would be) so, when he tied Myfanwy to a rock near the beach, he rolled up his trousers to the knees and jumped into the shallow water. Suddenly, he yelped in pain and Emma ran over to see what the matter was.

'Gramps, are you hurt?' said Emma anxiously.

'I've just trodden on a jelly fish,' said Grandpa, wincing in pain. 'It's never happened to me before and I'd no idea how painful it is,' he added.

'Gosh, Mr Davis,' said Laurie. 'Can we do anything to help?'

'Well, is that a truck I see on the coast road?' said Grandpa, squinting into the sun.

'Yes,' said Lizzy, who had the best eyesight. 'I think it's Farmer Williams.'

'Great, can you wave at him and ask him to stop?' asked Grandpa.

The girls and Pippa ran up to the road, waving and shouting, 'Farmer Williams, Richard, please stop!'

Richard stopped, looking concerned. 'Is anything wrong?'

'It's Grandpa,' said Emma. 'He's stung his foot badly on a jelly fish.'

Richard got out of the truck and walked down the beach to help Grandpa, who was limping along.

'So sorry to be a nuisance, Richard,' said Grandpa.

'Not at all,' said Richard. 'Delighted to help.'

'If you wouldn't mind driving me to the village chemist, that would be great,' said Grandpa.

'Shall I come with you, Gramps?' asked Emma.

'No, no, I wouldn't hear of it. You stay here and have a good time with your friends,' said Grandpa. 'After all, it's only a sting, even if it is painful. Please keep an eye on Myfanwy, though, until I come back for her.'

'Goodbye!' they called. 'Hope your foot's better soon.'

The girls returned to the beach where Laurie and Lizzy resumed their game of badminton, and Emma threw the ball for Pippa. She smiled as Pippa tripped over her paws in her haste to reach it. Emma looked up at the seagulls, who were calling to each other overhead. She noticed that there were now a few darker, more menacing clouds in the sky and the weather seemed to be on the turn. She shivered as the breeze picked up and became fresher. Emma noticed that Katie was missing.

'Where's Katie?' she called to Laurie and Lizzy. They stopped their game and looked around. They shook their heads in puzzlement. A cold hand seemed to encircle Emma's heart.

'Oh no, the lilo's gone too,' said Laurie.

'When was the last time anyone saw her?' asked Lizzy.

'I guess it was when Gramps was getting into Richard's truck,' said Emma.

'But look, if she was silly enough to take the lilo onto the sea, she's nowhere to be seen,' said Laurie, on the verge of tears.

'I guess she could've been swept out of the bay and round the headland,' said Emma. 'Lizzy, you're the fastest runner, can you run up there and look for Katie?'

Lizzy was already running up the cliff path as fast as her legs would take her. When she reached the top, she called in relief to Emma and Laurie 'I can see her, I can see her. She's on the lilo and it's just round the headland.' She turned to shout, 'Katie, don't panic, we'll rescue you. Hold on!'

'What on earth do we do now?' said Laurie in desperation.

'Pippa,' said Emma. 'Go up to the coast road and see if you can find someone to help us, but be careful of the cars.' Pippa gave a quick bark and ran off to try to find help. 'I guess there's only one option for us now and that's Myfanwy. Please, please, let Gramps have left the keys in the ignition.'

She and Laurie ran into the shallow water and hoisted themselves up into Myfanwy.

'Hooray, the keys are there,' said Emma in relief.

'But do you know how to drive her?' said Laurie.

'No,' said Emma, 'but we're going to have to learn very quickly!' With that, she unhooked the rope from the rock and turned the engine on. 'Hang on Laurie, we may be in for a bumpy ride.' Myfanwy lurched from one side to another and Emma attempted to steer her around the headland. The wind was starting to blow much harder now and the sea was becoming choppy.

'Katie, Katie, we're coming to get you!' cried Laurie.

Katie looked white with fear. She burst into tears when she saw Emma, Laurie and Myfanwy.

'What should we do now?' asked Emma. 'I can't control Myfanwy well enough to get close to the lilo.'

'I know,' said Laurie. 'Let's get as close as we dare and then I'll throw this rope over to Katie. She's a good swimmer and it's only a short distance.'

'Good thinking,' said Emma, who was beginning to get the hang of Myfanwy and had slowed her right down, inching her gently towards the lilo. 'I daren't get any nearer,' she said, as both the boat and lilo were now swaying with the tide. It had also started raining and the wind was fresh.

'Katie, listen to me,' said Laurie. 'Get in the water and swim. I'm throwing this rope into the water and, as soon as you swim to it, I'll pull you in.'

'I can't, I can't,' said a shivering, sobbing Katie. 'There may be sharks and I'm too scared.'

'Katie, you can do this. In fact, you must. Just pretend it's St David's swimming pool. It's hardly any distance at all, you know, and we're here!' cried Laurie.

'Yes, you can rely on us and Myfanwy,' said

Emma. 'Come on, Katie.'

Katie gave herself a shake, got into the water, but was still holding onto the lilo. The sea was now really choppy and a big wave washed over Katie's head. This made her cry harder. Even Myfanwy was rolling more violently from side to side.

'Come on, Katie,' urged Laurie and Emma. 'You've got to let go. It's only a few strokes to the rope. Please be quick before the sea gets even rougher.'

Sobbing, Katie started to swim to the rope, but she must have been too cold or scared to do it, and another big wave washed over her. Katie disappeared under the water.

'Katie, Katie!' shouted Emma in distress.

Laurie dived into the sea, hoisted Katie out of the water with her strong arms, and did backstroke to reach Myfanwy. Emma quickly helped lift Katie into the boat and then Laurie climbed in afterwards.

'Phew!' said Laurie. 'That was really scary.'

Katie was soaking wet, her fair hair plastered to her head, and she was shaking uncontrollably. Emma and Laurie were not sure whether this was because she was cold or in shock. Emma found Grandpa's jacket and wrapped it around Katie. She also found an old cardigan for Laurie.

'You're safe now, Katie,' said Emma, rubbing her thin arms.

'I'll look after Katie,' said Laurie. 'You start sailing Myfanwy and let's get back to calmer water as soon as we can.'

Emma turned the key in the ignition and Myfanwy didn't start. She tried again and the engine sputtered to a halt.

'Oh no!' cried Katie. 'How will we get back? We're doomed and it's all my fault.'

Even Laurie was starting to look worried.

Emma took a big breath. 'Come on, Myfanwy, you can do it,' she said, crossing her fingers. She turned the key in the ignition again and Myfanwy's engine started up. They looked at each other in relief. The ride was bumpy, but Emma did her very best to control Myfanwy, and they finally made their way back. By this time, Lizzy had run down the cliff path and was waiting anxiously on the beach. All three girls carried Katie back through the shallow water. They piled as many clothes onto her as they could.

'There's hot tea in the thermos flask in the picnic basket. There should be sugar cubes in there too. They should help with the shock,' said Emma. 'Try to get Katie warm and I'll go for help.' Emma ran up to the coast road and, much to her delight and amazement, saw Richard driving towards her with Pippa in the front passenger seat. 'Richard, oh thank goodness you're here!' cried Emma, who burst into tears in sheer relief.

'What is it?' asked Richard.

'It's Katie,' replied Emma. 'She was washed out to sea on the lilo and almost drowned.'

Richard ran down the beach and carried Katie back to the truck, gently placing her on the back seat. By now, the heavens had opened and they were all soaked to the skin in the torrential rain.

'Okay, everyone in,' said Richard. 'We're going straight to St David's hospital.'

Sometime later, Katie was tucked up in the children's ward for observation and her parents had arrived.

'I don't think there's any real cause for concern,' said Richard. 'Judging by what the doctor said, it's mainly shock. You all deserve medals for rescuing Katie. You were brilliant!'

'Thanks, Richard. I just wish one of us had noticed Katie taking the lilo out on the sea and stopped her,' said Lizzy, miserably.

'Thank goodness, Laurie got her Advanced Swimmer's badge recently,' said Emma.

'Yes, Laurie's a fantastic swimmer,' said Lizzy.

'How did Pippa tell you something was wrong?' said Laurie, blushing on account of all the praise.

'It was incredible really,' said Richard. 'I'd taken your Grandpa to the chemist and then driven him home. As I was driving back, I saw a black poodle

123

running towards me and thought it looked awfully like Pippa. I stopped the truck and she started barking excitedly at me. So, I got out of the truck and said, "Pippa, is that you? What is it?" At that, she looked at me reproachfully and, when I didn't move, she caught hold of the bottom of my trouser leg and wouldn't let go! For a moment, I thought she had taken leave of her senses, but then I realised that something bad must have happened. So, I got back into the truck with Pippa still hanging onto my trouser leg! When she realised I intended to drive back to the beach, mercifully she let go!'

'So, as usual, the real heroine of the tale is Pippa,' said Emma fondly, stroking her curly black head.

'Come along, now,' said Richard. 'Pippa isn't actually supposed to be in a hospital and you must be exhausted. Let's go home.'

They dropped off Lizzy and Laurie first. 'Oh no, Richard, what shall we do about Myfanwy and our things?' said Emma in concern.

'It's okay,' said Richard. 'I telephoned your grandfather from the hospital and he was going to collect Myfanwy and all your gear.'

'Phew,' said Emma. 'Richard, you think of everything.'

'My pleasure. After all, you did catch my egg thief,' he added, with a twinkle in his eye.

'Yes, how is the delightful Philip?' asked Emma with a grin. 'Is he still helping you?'

'He now has the makings of a promising farmer!' said Richard.

Katie was not really hurt, but only shocked and scared when she was released from hospital the next day. The following Saturday, the girls met up at the foot of Mabel. Emma with Pippa, Lizzy and Laurie arrived first and, lastly, Katie came, looking pale and forlorn.

'Katie, dearest, thank goodness you're safe and we still have you,' Emma said tearfully. They all put their arms around Katie, Pippa licked her leg and even Mabel seemed to lean forward to take part in the embrace. Katie was overwhelmed and started to cry.

'I'm so sorry I put you through that horrible ordeal with me,' she said. 'I can't imagine what I was thinking of. My mum told me I must promise her, you, and myself never to do that again.'

'Don't worry, we know you won't,' said Lizzy.

'Thank goodness you're such an amazing swimmer, Laurie, or else I would've drowned,' said Katie.

'Well, if you're thanking us all,' said Emma. 'Don't forget Myfanwy!'

'Or Pippa, for that matter,' said Laurie. 'I don't

think Richard has got over the shock of having a snapping Pippa dangling from his trousers!' They laughed, Pippa barked merrily and Mabel moved her branches back and forth, which made her leaves rustle in agreement.

The summer holidays were almost at an end and the sunshine changed to the beautiful light, which often appears between summer and autumn. Emma noticed that the sky was blue with a few tiny clouds high up – the trees were still green, but it now seemed that their tops had been brushed with gold and red.

The children were preparing to return to school. In Emma's case, she discovered she had grown taller. This meant taking the hem down on her school skirt. She hated needlework with a passion, but wished she had listened more intently to Miss Grigson. Then it would not have taken her so long.

The Grove Park Girls' school choir was practising hard for a momentous performance of Handel's Messiah with all the choirs of Wales in St Gwilym's Hall, Llandudno, scheduled for late October. So, between school work and choir rehearsals, Emma had practically no spare time for seeing her friends.

The great day finally dawned and Grandpa, Granny, Edward and Emma's three friends took the coach to Llandudno to hear the Handel. The performance was a huge success and Miss Prendergast was in her element. Anyone would have thought that she alone had been responsible for training all the Welsh choirs taking part, not just the choir of Grove Park girls' school!

'Girls, girls,' she said to them afterwards, with tears shining in her eyes. 'This has certainly been one of the beacons of my illustrious career!' At this, Emma pretended to look in her satchel in order to hide a smile.

Meanwhile, Grandpa had been making enquiries about a trumpet teacher for Edward. He'd discovered one in the form of Mr Atkinson, a peripatetic music teacher at St David's boys' school, who spent his holidays touring as the trumpeter in a jazz band that had a cult following in Romania.

More significantly, he was also lead trumpeter and the shining star of Miss Prendergast's brass band! In the autumn term, Edward started trumpet lessons with Mr Atkinson and real progress began to be made, at long last.

On the following Saturday, the girls met up as usual in Mabel's branches and congratulated Emma.

'That was really amazing, Emma,' said Katie, 'to have so many voices singing those wonderful tunes.'

'Yes,' said Lizzy, 'and you made Miss Prendergast a very happy woman.'

'The question is...' said Emma, '...will she ever stop preening and return to normality?'

'I wish I could sing properly,' said Laurie ruefully.

'Actually, you have a lovely voice,' said Emma, 'but you have to practise to be good.'

'Like a sportswoman,' said Katie. 'You wouldn't be such a great swimmer, Laurie, if you never practised.'

'In many ways though, I'm glad the concert is over,' said Emma. 'It was really difficult to think of anything else while the rehearsals were going on. Also, I'll be glad to see less of Miss Prendergast. She really upset Edward in the summer, you know. She could have let him down gently about the brass band; said he was too young or something, rather than telling him he was useless at the trumpet.'

'Yes, it was really nasty of her and totally unnecessary,' agreed Laurie.

'At times, old people don't seem to have learned anything from their life experiences, do they?' added Lizzy, thoughtfully.

'So, how's Edward getting along with Mr Atkinson?'

'Very well indeed,' said Emma. 'It just goes to show the difference good teaching can make, doesn't it?'

'Where does Ed have his lessons?' asked Laurie.

'Oh, sometimes Mr Atkinson comes to The

Syngret. Other times Ed goes to his house,' said Emma.

'Dishy, isn't he?' said Lizzy slyly. 'Now Richard will have a rival for your affections.'

'I can't imagine what you could possibly mean!' exclaimed Emma in high dudgeon.

They laughed and Mabel rustled her leaves.

Chapter Nine
The Detectives Investigate

The following Thursday after school, Emma was on her way to the village shop. As she and Pippa walked along Church Lane, she noticed that Philip Evans was standing outside St Mary Magdalene church, looking furtive. Emma slowed her pace and watched as Philip looked right and left and then went into the church.

'What on earth's he doing?' asked Emma. Pippa shook her head.

'Right, let's go and see.'

Emma marched up to the church and went in. Philip was the only person in there.

'What're you doing here, Philip?' said Emma belligerently.

'Woof,' said Pippa.

'What am I doing here?' said Philip sounding cross. 'Actually, I came to find my mum although she must've already finished cleaning the church. I might ask what you're doing here as well as that horrible little dog of yours?'

'How dare you insult my poodle!' said Emma, tossing her red curls. 'I wouldn't be a bit surprised if it was you who stole the teapot with the roof money in it!'

'Why don't you try to prove it?' said Philip spitefully.

'Come along, Pippa,' said Emma 'I, for one, have had enough of this horrible boy!' and, with that, Emma and Pippa stormed out of the church.

'Pippa, my intuition tells me it was definitely Philip Evans who stole the teapot,' said Emma, 'but how can we prove it?'

Pippa shook her head in bemusement.

Emma spent the next couple of nights tossing and turning, wondering how to find the evidence necessary to prove Philips Evans' guilt. The following Saturday, she met her friends, as usual, in Mabel's branches.

'So, you see,' said Emma. 'I'm convinced that Philip's our thief, but we need to find the evidence against him.'

'That's all very well, Emma,' said Lizzy, 'but this could be nothing more than a hunch.'

'I can't help agreeing with Emma,' said Laurie.

'We know that Philip Evans is a nasty piece of work and has already proved himself a thief. It must be much more tempting to steal lots of money than a few eggs!'

'So, what I propose is this,' said Emma, taking a deep breath. 'We need to search Philip's bedroom to try to find the teapot or the money!'

All three girls looked shocked and started talking at once.

'Hang on a minute,' said Lizzy. 'I don't think we can break the law to prove Philip's the thief.'

'Yes, we'd be just as bad as him!' said Katie.

'Well, to be fair,' said Laurie. 'We wouldn't be as bad as Philip because we wouldn't steal anything. We'd just be looking for evidence.'

'The police might not see it that way,' pointed out Lizzy.

'Look, Philip's Dad works in Colwyn on Saturdays and Philip will be working for Richard at Fairdale farm. We just have to wait until his Mum goes out shopping and then break in,' said Emma.

'How would we do that?' said Katie.

'Don't you remember – I still have Philip's lock pick?' said Emma with a laugh.

'It would be rich to use Philip's own lock pick to break into his house!' said Laurie, her dark eyes twinkling with merriment.

'So, you propose we search Philip's house during

the daytime rather than waiting until it's dark?' said Lizzy.

'Personally, I think that's the best bet,' said Emma. 'The most important thing is to break in when we know they'll be out. In any case, their bungalow's on the edge of the village and they don't have any neighbours.'

'Okay, but can you open a door with the lock pick?' asked Laurie.

'I've spent the last two evenings until late into the night practising on my bedroom door and I think I've cracked it,' said Emma proudly.

'In that case, let's aim for next Saturday morning,' said Laurie.

'Oh my goodness,' said Katie faintly.

'Okay, if we're doing this, then we need to plan it properly,' said Emma. 'Laurie and Katie, you have your bikes so one of you can be on surveillance at Fairdale farm to make sure Philip doesn't come back and the other can follow Philip's mum to the shop.'

'I'll watch over the charming Philip, if you like,' volunteered Laurie.

'And Lizzy, you can keep lookout when I go into the house,' said Emma.

'That seems a good plan,' said Laurie.

'Are we all agreed, then?' asked Emma.

'Agreed,' said Laurie and Lizzy firmly.

'Are you with us, Katie?' asked Laurie.

Katie gulped and then said, 'I'm not sure this is a good idea, but of course I'm with you. Aren't we the Four Musketeers, come what may?'

'Five, including Pippa,' corrected Emma.

The following Saturday, the girls met up at 9am in the field next to Philip Evans' bungalow. They looked solemn and, in particular, Katie seemed very pale. Mr Evans had driven off to work, as his car wasn't there, and Philip had already gone to Fairdale farm. Laurie and Katie had their bicycles with them. They lay down in the long grass under an oak tree to wait until Mrs Evans went out shopping.

'I do hope she didn't go shopping yesterday evening instead!' said Lizzy drily.

Fortunately, after about twenty minutes, the front door opened and Mrs Evans came out of the house, unlocked her bicycle and got on it. As soon as she'd left, the girls sprang into action.

'I promise to be in the house for half an hour only,' said Emma.

'And Pippa and I will keep watch for you outside,' said Lizzy.

'I'm off to follow Mrs Evans and I'll race back here if she shows any sign of leaving the shop within thirty minutes,' said Katie, getting on her bike.

'And I'm going to Richard's farm to make sure, by hook or by crook, that Philip doesn't come back within the next half hour,' said Laurie.

The girls knew what they had to do and Laurie and Katie sped away on their bikes in different directions.

'Lizzy, what do you think?' said Emma. 'I can't see anyone, can you?'

'No, I think the coast's clear,' said Lizzy.

Emma had already put on her thin rubber gloves, so she brought out the lock pick, placed it in the lock of the front door and moved it from one side to the other several times – but the door didn't open.

'Blast,' said Emma. 'This is much more difficult than my bedroom door.'

'What a pity if we can't open the door, after all this,' whispered Lizzy. 'Quick, hide, there's a car driving along the road.' With that, they ran back into the long grass.

'Phew,' said Emma. 'That was close. Okay, I'll try again.'

So, once again, she tried the pick in the lock of the front door with Lizzy and Pippa looking anxiously about them. This time, they heard a click. Emma turned the door handle and was in the house. She quickly looked around and spotted Philip's bedroom immediately because posters of Liverpool star footballers in action were plastered over the walls.

*

Meanwhile, Laurie had arrived at Fairdale Farm and taken cover behind a hedge, watching Philip through her dad's binoculars, which she had borrowed without asking him! About ten minutes later, Philip slipped and fell into a pile of cow manure, and Laurie had to stop herself laughing out loud. But she immediately became very serious when she saw Philip go up to Richard and gesticulate towards his trousers. Richard nodded and Philip set off towards his bicycle. Laurie realised, with a sinking heart, that Richard had agreed that Philip could go home to change.

'Oh no,' said Laurie to herself. 'Emma hasn't had nearly enough time yet to search the house.' She quickly got on her own bicycle with the aim of delaying Philip. 'Philip, Philip, wait!' she called.

Philip slowed down on his bicycle and looked around. 'What do you want?' he asked.

'I couldn't be sure it was you,' said Laurie, desperately trying to think of what to say to him. 'How are you getting on with Richard?'

'Are you having a laugh?' scowled Philip, turning to leave.

'Oh, Philip, what happened to your trousers?' said Laurie in pretend amazement.

'What does it look like?' said Philip. 'I fell into a heap of manure and I'm going home to change.'

'Oh, you poor thing,' said Laurie. 'What else do

you get up to on the farm?'

'Has anyone ever told you how irritating you are?' asked Philip, turning to leave.

At this point, Laurie realised that drastic action was necessary and she pretended to lose control of her bike and drove it into Philip's front wheel. They both fell into the road.

'Just what're you doing? Have you gone raving mad?' shouted Philip.

'I'm so sorry, Philip. I don't know what happened there. I just seemed to lose control. Of course, I'm not the best cyclist in the world,' said Laurie, rubbing her knee ruefully. 'Anyway, are you all right? Do tell me I didn't hurt you.'

'I'm fine, but will you just please go away?' said Philip in exasperation.

Laurie couldn't think of any more delaying tactics, so the only thing she could do was to follow Philip back to his house. She gave a huge sigh of relief and slowed down when she rounded the bend and saw Lizzy and Emma in the field outside Philip's bungalow.

'You!' said Philip in exasperation. 'What're you both doing outside my house?'

'Well actually, we're just going for a walk,' said Lizzy coolly.

'Any objection?' asked Emma.

'I tell you what, this one is completely off her

rocker!' said Philip, pointing at Laurie who was just getting off her bike.

'Charming,' said Emma. 'You may want to change your trousers, Philip. They do seem extremely smelly!' They laughed.

Philip unlocked his front door and slammed it shut. By this time, Katie had arrived on her bike.

'Come on, quick,' said Emma and they raced off to Mabel with Katie and Laurie on their bikes.

'What happened to your knee, Laurie?' said Lizzy. 'It's bleeding.'

'Oh, it's not too bad' said Laurie bravely. 'Philip fell in some manure and Farmer Richard gave him permission to go home and change his trousers, so I had to come up with delaying tactics very quickly. When I'd run out of things to say, I drove my bike into his!'

'Goodness, how brave you are,' said Katie admiringly. 'Luckily, Mrs Evans was so slow in the village shop that I didn't have to do anything. At the rate she was going, she'll be there all day!'

'Anyway, Emma,' said Lizzy in excitement. 'What did you find in the house?'

'Absolutely nothing,' said Emma sadly. 'I looked in every drawer and cupboard in Philip's bedroom. I found lots of dirty, smelly old socks but no cash and no sign of the teapot. I even came across Philip's post office account book and could see he'd made deposits with the egg money until March, but zilch after that.'

'Oh dear,' said Laurie in dismay. 'Does that mean Philip's innocent, after all?'

'What a disappointment!' exclaimed Katie.

'Well then,' said Lizzy reasonably. 'We'll just have to take it philosophically and eliminate Philip from the list of suspects.'

'Ha! I won't be eliminating him just yet!' cried Emma.

Chapter Ten

Hallowe'en

The days became colder and darker, clouds scudded across the sky and the wind blew around piles of bronzed and burnished leaves. Granny described it as 'witching weather' and the children's thoughts turned to the Hallowe'en party that Granny and Grandpa held every year.

'Goodness, what on earth shall I wear?' said Emma.

'Luckily, I'm okay,' said Edward. 'I can wear the bat costume I made for the cub scouts' gala in the summer. In fact, I may make a costume for Pippa so that she can be my bat poodle!'

'I'll be in my spider's costume and your grandpa will be a vampire, as usual,' said Granny.

'I may invest in a new wig and fangs this year,' said Grandpa thoughtfully.

'I must say St David's fancy dress shop has

become very expensive,' said Granny. 'If you want a new costume, darling, why don't you visit those funny little shops in the high street one Saturday? I'll bet you could pick up a wonderful bargain.'

'That's a great idea, Granny, thanks,' said Emma.

So, the following Saturday, the girls met at the foot of Mabel but, instead of climbing her branches, they walked down the country lane next to St Mary Magdalene's church, past the Splash, paying their respects to the ducks and geese en-route, and finally into St David's High Street.

'I hope Mabel won't feel neglected,' said Katie.

'I'm sure she'll understand,' said Laurie.

'Really, I don't know why we're looking for Hallowe'en ideas in local shops,' noted Lizzy acerbically, 'when the teachers at our school kindly provide so much inspiration!'

'I guess we could take a leaf out of Cynthia's book and dye our hair blue!' said Laurie.

'Gosh, aren't we being nasty?' said Katie guiltily.

'Let's go into this shop, Hatty J's,' said Emma. 'It's very good value and it's more unique than some of the others.'

They went inside and looked at the clothes.

'I love this purple velvet cloak,' said Lizzy, her grey eyes lighting up. 'It's very reasonably priced and will go really well over my costume.'

'And look what I've found,' said Emma, delightedly. 'A cat mask which ties round the back of your head with a ribbon. It's even got fantastic whiskers!'

'Oh, do try it on,' said Katie, clapping her hands.

'It fits perfectly,' said Laurie.

Having paid for their purchases, they left the shop, chattering happily.

'I know – to get us in the Hallowe'en mood, let's walk back along Broomstick Lane,' said Laurie.

'It's such a great name,' said Lizzy. 'I wonder how it came by it.'

'Who knows,' said Emma, 'but it's certainly atmospheric.'

'Most of these houses are huge,' said Katie as a gust of wind lifted up a heap of golden leaves and tossed them into the air. 'Do you think just one family lives in each of them?'

'Yes, particularly if that family has the name Dracula!' said Laurie with a chuckle.

'Just look at this one,' said Lizzy as they passed a particularly large and forbidding house. 'It really is like Count Dracula's castle. It should definitely have vampire bats circling round its turrets!' said Lizzy.

'Perhaps it does, at the midnight hour,' declared Emma, attempting a witch's cackle.

'Have you actually seen Dracula, then?' asked

Katie, in wonder. 'My mum would never let me watch that.'

'I can't say my Mum actually let me watch it,' said Lizzy, 'but I sneaked downstairs to watch on TV one night, when Mum and Dad had gone to bed. It's lucky they're such heavy sleepers. I must admit Dracula was really scary and I couldn't sleep for ages. Afterwards I rather wished I hadn't seen it.'

By this time, they were approaching Mabel and the parting of the ways.

'Great,' said Emma. 'I look forward to seeing you next Saturday in your costumes.'

'Your grandparents are such fun,' said Laurie.

'I know,' said Emma, happily.

When Emma and Pippa returned to The Syngret, Granny and Grandpa were in the kitchen. Emma was about to call out to them when she realised they were in the middle of a serious conversation and so she hesitated to interrupt. She was about to go up to her room, but stayed to listen outside the kitchen when she realised what was being discussed.

'I just don't see how we're going to manage, Edie,' said Grandpa. 'The final straw is that the windows need replacing and we don't have the money for it.'

'But then, what shall we do?' said Granny.

'I know it would be a terrible wrench to leave the

Syngret,' said Grandpa hesitatingly, 'but it would mean that we would have a pot of money at our disposal. Apart from the windows, poor old Major Beetroot's not going to last forever.'

'Oh no, Ernest,' said Granny tremulously. 'I just couldn't bear the idea of leaving The Syngret. I know it's stupid to become so attached to a house, but we've lived here since we were married, and the house is part of the family. I would rather take in lodgers, really I would.'

'Don't upset yourself, Edie,' said Grandpa, putting his arm round her. 'We'll just have to hope it doesn't come to that.'

At this point, Emma could bear it no longer and burst into the kitchen.

'Oh, Granny, Gramps, are you really thinking of selling The Syngret? It'd be so terrible!'

'Emma,' said Grandpa sternly. 'Have you been listening at the keyhole?'

At that, Emma started to cry, saying, 'No, I just couldn't help hearing what you were saying.'

'Don't worry, Emma,' said Granny, wiping a tear from her own eye. 'Things are not as bad as that yet. We're not selling The Syngret for the time being. Now let's forget all about it and think about our Hallowe'en party instead!'

'Okay,' said Emma, still looking a bit shocked, and she and Pippa went upstairs to her room.

Emma sat on her bed and Pippa jumped up to lick her nose. Emma felt that recent events were rushing through her head like a kaleidoscope and, as her thoughts cleared, a truly appalling suspicion came to her. Who was worried about being hard up and who had a key to the church? She had been so convinced that the teapot thief was Philip Evans, but how could she have been blind enough not to realise that Grandpa was the number one suspect? She had started the detection project and rejoiced in the Case of the Missing Teapot, never dreaming that her actions might lead to the arrest and imprisonment of her beloved Gramps.

A sleepless night followed, but by the morning, Emma was able to give herself a good shake.

'Pippa,' said Emma. 'How could I ever suspect Gramps of anything criminal? Of course, he'd never steal the church repair fund for any reason in the whole world.' Pippa nodded her head in agreement.

The following Saturday, The Syngret was bustling with activity. Granny and Emma were on punch duty (a fruity version for children and an alcoholic one for the grown-ups), Edward attempted to vacuum the carpet with the help of Pippa, and Grandpa brought down the Hallowe'en decorations from the attic to adorn the old house. A huge, grey spider's web covered one wall, bats dangled from ceilings, pumpkins appeared in the strangest of places and a witch doll on a broomstick appeared over the front door. Grandpa had secretly called her 'Hilda' after a certain relative! He had also hollowed out several real pumpkins and carved faces into them. They looked extremely effective with a candle inside each one, and they were placed on tables and windowsills, with the largest pumpkin on top of the piano. Myfanwy, who was parked by the caravan round the back of the house, had not been forgotten and sported a witch's hat!

After Granny had finished cutting up fruit for the punch, she got out her enormous casserole pot, in the shape of a witch's cauldron, and embarked upon her (in)famous, Hallowe'en sausage stew.

'My goodness, I think I'm getting too old for all this,' said Granny.

'Rubbish,' said Grandpa. 'You'll never be too old for anything, Edie,' and he gave her a fond kiss.

By 6pm, everything was in readiness and there was just time to dash upstairs to put on their costumes. Granny was a very effective silvery spider, as she was so slender, and she helped Emma to tie on her cat mask. Grandpa was looking particularly ghastly as a vampire, with a chalk white face, fangs, and fake blood. He helped Edward to adjust his bat costume and bat mask, and then they helped Pippa into her bat wings.

'We really put the Addams family to shame!' exclaimed Grandpa, proudly.

Just at that moment, the cuckoo sounded to indicate that the first guests had arrived, and they ushered in Laurie in her pumpkin hat, Lizzy in her glamorous, purple velvet cloak and Katie in her black fairy outfit. Edward took them over to the far end of the living room to bob for apples. Emma was on front door service and opened the door to welcome Farmer Richard as a friendly looking Count Dracula and Angela Barnard as the bride of Dracula, wearing an old wedding dress with a few Hallowe'en twists, such as a bat affixed to her shoulder and an intricate cobweb decorating the foot of the dress.

'Happy Hallowe'en, Emma *bach*,' twinkled Richard.

'How lovely to see you, Richard – and Miss Barnard, of course,' said Emma. 'We do hope you'll sing for us later, Richard.'

The cuckoo sounded once again and Emma opened the door, this time to find Colonel Granger, the pompous local councillor, resplendent as Frankenstein's monster with a bolt through his neck!

'Ah, Emma, good evening to you,' he said. 'I hope I'm not late, but urgent work kept me in the office until now. I'm so very busy, you know. Not that I begrudge working on a Saturday, you understand, when my work is of such importance to the community. However, I do feel that, as one of the most respected and well-known figures in St David's, I should also mingle with the populace at large,' he added officiously. Having given him a glass of punch, she could contain herself no longer and shut herself in the kitchen to have a hearty laugh at his expense.

'I don't know how he does it,' she said to Pippa, 'but that man manages to be totally self-important and humourless even with a plastic bolt through his neck!'

At this stage, Emma's services as accompanist were required to play the piano for Richard who sang 'The Foggy, Foggy Dew' to tumultuous applause. He then sang unaccompanied the ghostly Irish folk song 'She moved through the fair' and, when he sang the last verse, the audience was enthralled, and silence reigned:

> *Last night she came to me,*
> *My dead love came in.*
> *So softly she came That her feet made no din.*
> *As she laid her hand on me,*
> *And this she did say:*
> *It will not be long, love,*
> *'Til our wedding day.*

After he had stopped singing, the spell lasted for ages and then people started clapping, cheering and stamping their feet.

'Ah, Richard, it's such a pleasure to hear you,' said Grandpa, thrusting a glass of punch into his hand.

'Yes, how lucky we are to have such a fantastic singer in our midst,' said Granny with tears in her eyes.

Much to her consternation, Emma noticed that, shortly afterwards, Colonel Granger had monopolised Richard in an attempt to coerce him into singing for the inauguration of a deadly dull rotary club event. 'Such a worthy cause, my boy!' bellowed Colonel Granger patronisingly, slapping Richard on the back.

'Actually, just at the moment, my time's taken up with my farm and my oratorio commitments,' said Richard. 'Do excuse me for a moment, I must just speak to Peter Jones over there,' and he made a hasty getaway.

'Oh, goodness,' whispered Emma to Lizzy. 'I do hope Colonel Granger doesn't put Richard off coming to our parties. I can't imagine who invited him anyway. Granny and Gramps can't stand him.'

The party was soon in full swing and two teams were trying, against the clock, to wrap up one of their team members as an Egyptian Mummy, using toilet paper for the purpose!

'Are you having a good time, dear Katie?' asked Emma.

'Oh, it's wonderful,' said Katie, with her blue eyes shining. 'I think it's even better than last year.'

'Yes,' said Laurie, her dark eyes sparkling merrily. 'Apart from anything, it's so funny seeing people in their costumes.'

'You can say that again,' agreed Lizzy. 'Have you seen Colonel Granger?'

'Yes and I can honestly say the sight will haunt me forever!' exclaimed Emma.

'Who's that over there, wearing the bird of prey mask?' asked Lizzy.

'No idea, as you can't see his face,' said Laurie. 'I'll go over and ask him.'

By then, the old house was rocking to the sound of 'The Monster Mash' by Bobby Pickett and the Crypt-kickers, so the three girls weren't able to hear a word of what Laurie said to the bird of prey.

Laurie returned, looking puzzled. 'I congratulated him on his mask and asked who he was, but he just shook his head and moved away,' she said. 'You know, that mask's pretty creepy. It's the only costume I've seen so far that definitely hasn't been funny.'

'Oh, never mind,' said Lizzy. 'Take no notice of

him if he wants to be mysterious.'

'Yes, let's concentrate on the costumes that are fun,' said Katie.

By this time, many of the adults were looking tipsy, several wigs were adrift, the mad monk had knocked over a pumpkin with his cassock, and Colonel Granger's plastic bolt had now migrated to his head at the wrong angle. A spooky conga wove around the garden and someone snatched away Myfanwy's witch hat and placed it on top of the greenhouse, next to the trilby.

'Oh dear,' said Laurie. 'I see the grown-ups are getting out of hand.'

'Yes, this might well end in tears and they'll feel embarrassed afterwards,' said Katie thoughtfully.

'That's if they can remember what they did afterwards,' said Lizzy acerbically.

'Pippa, have you seen Edward?' said Emma. Pippa shook her head in puzzlement. Emma had a look in the living and dining rooms and then tried the kitchen, all to no avail. 'Have any of you seen Edward?' she asked.

'Not for a while,' replied Laurie.

'I can't honestly remember when I last saw him,' said Lizzy.

'He was handing out the ghostly vol-au-vents at one point,' said Katie.

'I'm beginning to feel worried,' said Emma.

'Go and look in the other rooms before you start panicking,' said Laurie practically, so that's what Emma did. She came downstairs and shook her head in response to their quizzical looks.

'I've checked everywhere, even the cellar, and he's not there. What shall we do?' asked Emma.

'Why don't we have a look in the garden before alerting the adults?' said Lizzy.

'Yes, perhaps his bat costume got caught on a bush,' said Laurie.

'Very possibly,' said Katie.

'Come on, everyone,' said Emma, relieved to be taking action. 'Pippa can be our sniffer dog.'

They went out into the garden and checked in the garage and the greenhouse.

'Edward, where are you?' called Laurie loudly.

'If this is a joke, Edward, it isn't funny and I'll be angry with you,' said Emma.

'Perhaps he got fed up with the party and went in the caravan,' said Lizzy.

They opened the caravan door but it was in darkness.

Shortly afterwards, they reached the swings at the very end of the garden, still calling in vain for Edward.

'He isn't anywhere in the garden,' said Emma, nearly in tears.

'Let's have a look down the lane,' said Katie. 'He might have sprained his ankle or something'.

So, they went into the lane calling, 'Edward, where are you?'

'Gosh, that's a very grand Jaguar!' exclaimed Lizzy. 'Whose is it?'

'Oh, I think it belongs to the ever-modest Colonel Granger,' said Emma.

'I guess he must be very rich then,' said Katie.

'I don't know,' said Laurie. 'My dad says you can never tell about people – sometimes they borrow money to show off and the next thing you know, they've gone bankrupt.'

'I hate to say this,' said Lizzy, 'and, of course, I don't want to put the fear of God up you unnecessarily...' she added, hesitantly.

'What is it?' asked Emma.

'It's just that I recall the bird of prey disappeared at about the same time as Edward – at least, I remember seeing them both when the ghostly vol-au-vents were being handed round and I don't remember seeing either since.'

'Are you suggesting that the bird of prey's got Edward?' asked Laurie in dismay.

'I'm just thinking out loud really,' said Lizzy, apologetically.

'The bird of prey may well just have gone home,' remarked Katie prosaically.

'I must admit, though, I did have a really bad feeling about that bird of prey,' said Laurie anxiously.

'I guess we should go back to the house and tell Granny and Gramps,' said Emma. 'What an awful end to the evening.'

Just at that moment, the strains of 'Moon River' played on a trumpet, reached them. They only heard the first couple of lines and then the sound suddenly stopped.

'That's Edward's trumpet!' exclaimed Emma excitedly.

'And it's coming from the church,' said Katie.

They ran as fast as their costumes would allow and reached St Mary Magdalene in record time. The church itself was dark and quiet, but Pippa started to bark excitedly and ran round to the door of the beautiful stone bell tower.

'They must be up there,' shouted Laurie. The door was jammed shut and all four girls had to heave to get it open.

'Just a moment,' whispered Emma. 'We may need a weapon.' She looked around for inspiration.

They all looked on the ground and Laurie found a piece of thick tree branch.

'Here's a piece of wood,' said Laurie. 'That'll have to do as a club.'

They looked at each other, took a deep breath, and then Emma led the way up the steep, narrow wooden stairs to the ringing chamber. The bell ropes were hanging down so that the village's bell-ringers could ring the huge, cast iron bells above. As soon as they reached the ringing chamber with its wooden beams, they saw Edward and the bird of prey. Edward was sitting on the floor, crying softly to himself, with a sore red eye. As soon as he saw them, Edward ran across to Emma and started sobbing loudly.

'Edward, darling, are you hurt?' she asked.

By this time, the bird of prey was backing into the corner as Lizzy, Laurie and Katie approached him fiercely. At that moment, Pippa launched herself at the bird of prey's ankles, snarling fiercely.

'Ouch, get off me, you accursed dog,' said a boy's voice.

The girls looked at each other in amazed recognition and Laurie strode up to him and snatched off his mask. 'Philip Evans, I might have guessed,' she said contemptuously, her dark eyes flashing.

'What on earth do you think you were doing, kidnapping an innocent child?' asked Lizzy angrily.

'You are the lowest of the low,' added gentle Katie, roused to fury by such cowardly malevolence.

'I didn't kidnap Edward,' said Philip indignantly. 'I only wanted to scare you to get my own back. It's all your fault I've had to work so hard for Farmer

Williams every Saturday.'

'We'll soon see what the adults have to say about this,' said Emma, and with that they all started hauling on the nearest bell rope. The sound of St Mary Magdalene's magnificent bell rang out across the surrounding area – loud and pure and resonant.

As soon as he heard the sound, Philip realised that his hour of reckoning was fast approaching. He dashed down the wooden stairs, out of the main door, and across the field as fast as his legs could take him. In what seemed like no time, they heard the sound of a police siren, and Grandpa, Granny and Richard, looking grim and worried, had arrived with Constable Roberts. The girls stopped swinging on the bell and sat down on the floor. They seemed rather pale and shocked.

'Edward, speak to me,' said Emma. 'Are you okay?'

'It was really horrible,' said Edward, sobbing. 'I didn't know who he was. I thought he was going to kill me. When he ran down to lock the main door, I quickly pulled the tape off my mouth, got my trumpet and started to play "Moon River". He must have realised that people would hear, so he came back and knocked it out of my hand as quickly as he could. The trumpet hit me in the face.' With that, Edward cried harder than ever.

'That was really clever of you,' said Lizzy kindly.

'Yes, well done,' echoed Laurie and Katie.

'My darlings, are you all right?' said Granny tremulously, arriving in the bell loft. She was followed by Grandpa, Richard and Constable Roberts. 'Your grandfather and I realised something was wrong when we heard the bell. When we saw that you all had disappeared from the party, we realised it was a call for help.'

'So, we called Constable Roberts immediately and then set off for the belfry,' added Grandpa, looking anxious.

'We're so pleased to see you,' said Emma gravely. 'Poor Edward was kidnapped by Philip Evans so has had a very bad scare. That horrible boy managed to hurt Edward when he knocked his trumpet away.'

At this, Constable Roberts looked very serious indeed.

'Did any of you see where Philip ran off to?' he asked.

'Yes,' said Laurie. 'He ran across Waterdown Meadow, but we didn't see where he went after that.'

'Constable Roberts, we think Philip may also have stolen the church roof repair fund,' blurted out Emma. 'We caught him red-handed stealing Farmer Richard's eggs.'

Constable Roberts looked in surprise at Richard.

'It's true,' said Richard. 'Emma's completely right. He did steal my eggs.

'Goodness, Emma,' said Granny. 'You certainly kept that in the dark.'

'Well, when we've got him in custody, I'll interrogate him,' said Constable Roberts. With that, he drove off in his police car with the siren blaring.

'Children, the sooner we get you home the better,' said Grandpa. 'I'm taking Edward to Accident and Emergency so a doctor can take a look at his face and Richard's very kindly offered to drive the rest of you home.'

'Oh thank you, Richard,' said Emma. 'You always seem to come to our rescue, like our guardian angel,' she added tearfully. She went over, placed her hand on the bell rope, looked up at the huge bell and whispered, 'Thank you, Master Thomas, for helping us in our hour of need. What a wonderful bell you are.'

With that, Grandpa and Edward set off in Major Beetroot to St David's Accident and Emergency, and Richard drove everyone else home.

The next day, a pale and pensive family met around the breakfast table. Granny and Grandpa had placed a packet of frozen peas on Edward's face and tied it securely around the back of his head during the night in the hope of minimising the bruising. However, despite this precaution, the left side of his face was now purple and blue.

'How are you, my darling boy?' asked Granny.

'I'm okay, thanks, Granny,' said Edward, 'but I guess I won't be playing the trumpet for a few days.'

'The doctor assured us no permanent damage has been caused to Edward's eye or face,' said Grandpa.

'I just can't believe that horrible Philip Evans could kidnap a small boy like Edward in the first place. What a wicked, wicked thing to do,' said Granny.

'Thank goodness Emma, Pippa and friends were there to save the day,' said Grandpa with a smile.

'Yes, but what I don't understand, my darling girl...' said Granny, passing round tea and toast. '...is why you didn't come and tell us as soon as you noticed Edward was missing?'

'We thought perhaps his costume got caught on a tree in the garden and he was stuck. We were looking for him for ages and we did begin to suspect something awful had happened, but it wasn't until we heard him play "Moon River" on the trumpet that we recognised it as a call for help and dashed down to the church,' explained Emma.

'So, what exactly did happen, Ed?' said Grandpa, pulling Edward onto his knee.

'Well, Gramps,' said Edward, stuffing toast and marmalade into his mouth. 'After I'd passed round the ghostly vol-au-vents, a tall boy wearing a mask like an eagle came over to me and said he'd heard I was a very good trumpet-player and could I show him my trumpet. I'd no idea who he was but, as you can imagine, I was very proud and pleased he knew about my trumpet. So, I went to find it and he asked if I could play him something, but he said we'd better go outside or we'd disrupt the party. We did and it was then that he became really nasty, stuck a big piece of tape over my mouth and said I was going to come with him. So, he marched me down the lane to the church. I really tried to wriggle free, Grandpa, but he was too strong for me.' With this, he burst into tears and buried his head in Grandpa's shirt.

'There, there, dear boy, don't upset yourself,' said Grandpa, patting Edward's shoulder and wiping his eyes for him. 'It's all over now.'

'I think the very worst thing was I didn't know what he wanted, or why he was taking me away. He didn't say anything and I couldn't even ask him. I couldn't see his face, only his scary eagle mask. It was like a nightmare.

When we got to the church, he took me up to the bell tower and then ran down to lock the main door. That's when I ripped the tape off my mouth and took my chance to play 'Moon River'. Then he ran back up the stairs and knocked the trumpet out of my hand.'

'All I can say is thank heavens we were outside The Syngret and could hear your trumpet,' said Emma, shuddering at the thought of Edward being kept against his will in the bell tower for even longer.

'My darling boy,' said Granny. 'Thank goodness you had your trumpet with you. I'll never complain about it again!'

At that moment, the telephone owl hooted and Grandpa picked it up. 'Hello, Constable Roberts,' he said and their serious conversation lasted for a considerable time.

'So, have they arrested him?' asked Granny eagerly, as soon as Grandpa put down the phone.

'Yes, apparently. Philip sprained his ankle and Constable Roberts found him in a ditch at the far end of Waterdown Meadow. He was covered in manure! Constable Roberts said they had to hose him down at the station and he needs to have his car fumigated!' This was the first time any of them had laughed since Edward's kidnap.

'According to Constable Roberts, Philip kept on sniffling and saying he'd not intended to hurt Edward. Anyway, the police informed Philip's father who's absolutely furious and will probably make Philip's life a living hell from now on.'

'Presumably, the case will go to court?' said Granny. 'I think Philip is fifteen.'

'Well, according to Constable Roberts, the

charges are likely to be false imprisonment and the case could go to a juvenile court – but as no real harm was done and it's Philip's first offence, he is more likely to get a stiff talking to.'

'If that's so,' cried Granny. 'I think it much too lenient.'

Pippa barked in agreement.

'The only thing is, Emma,' said Grandpa. 'Constable Roberts doesn't think Philip could have stolen the teapot and church roof repair fund, as he was away on holiday in July with his Mum and Dad when the theft took place.'

'Really? I can hardly believe it,' said Emma, looking crestfallen.

'Oh please, let's stop thinking about that horrible boy,' said Edward. 'Who's for a game of Cluedo?' And that's what they did instead.

Chapter Eleven

Broomsticks Ahoy!

In early December, at a meeting with her friends in Mabel's branches, Emma asked them whether they would like to go carol singing.

'Of course, we can practise at The Syngret first with the piano before we try any of the carols unaccompanied.'

'Yes, it'll be great fun,' said Lizzy enthusiastically.

'And we can dress up with tinsel and make lanterns with candles to add to the atmosphere,' said Katie, her eyes sparkling.

'To be honest, I'm not sure. I just don't know that I can sing well enough,' said Laurie.

'I don't know why you're so lacking in confidence about your singing,' said Emma. 'You've got a lovely voice.'

'Why don't we try to raise money for the church roof?' said Laurie excitedly. 'I know that people won't be able to give enough to cover all the money that was stolen.'

'Yes, if we do that, perhaps we can inspire some of the adults to fund-raise, too,' said Emma. 'I think that's a great idea, Laurie.'

'Mmm, I can't help thinking that Father Pritchard doesn't deserve our efforts after being such an idiot, but the church does need a new roof,' said Lizzy thoughtfully.

'So, are we agreed?' said Emma. 'Agreed,' said one and all.

'Do you realise it's nearly Christmas and we're no closer to solving the Case of the Missing Teapot?' said Emma. 'It's so depressing that Philip seems to have an alibi for when the teapot was stolen.'

After several practice sessions at The Syngret, accompanied by a few well-timed barks from Pippa and much general merriment, they decided upon their repertoire of carols for the great event and had their lanterns (*i.e.* candles in jam jars) ready.

'Now, you must be careful,' said Granny, who was feeling apprehensive about the project. 'Please don't go into anyone's house, however nice they seem, and do take your whistles with you, in case of emergency.'

'Don't worry, Edie, I think they'll be all right. There are four of them, you know, plus one ferocious poodle!' said Grandpa.

Friday evening arrived and they congregated at The Syngret. The girls' colour scheme was green and gold, and Pippa was wearing her green tartan winter coat with gold tinsel tied around her neck and tail! Even the candles in their lanterns were gold and green, and they had a golden jam jar stating that any donations would be given to the church roof fund.

'You look so festive. I'll just take a photo,' said Emma, getting her camera out of her bag.

'You're so lucky to have a camera, Emma,' said Laurie.

'I know. Mum and Dad gave it to me as a special present when they left for Cyprus,' said Emma.

Lizzy stood in the middle and picked up Pippa so she could be centre stage in the photo.

'Where shall we start singing?' said Katie.

'Gosh, we've been concentrating so hard on practising, we never thought of that, did we?!' exclaimed Laurie.

'I think we should start with Broomstick Lane,' said Emma. 'Those houses are enormous so the people must be rich and will have lots of money to throw around!'

'That's all very well,' said Lizzy, 'but those houses are so big they might not actually hear us!'

'We do have to begin somewhere,' said Katie pragmatically. 'So let's start off at Broomstick Lane and we can always go elsewhere if need be.'

*

They walked down Church Lane, past St Mary Magdalene and the Splash, turned into St David's High Street and then into Broomstick Lane, which was looking dark and forbidding. They came to the first house which was well lit.

'Which carol shall we start with first?' said Laurie.

'How about 'Ding Dong Merrily on High'?' said Lizzy. 'That's a jolly one.'

Emma gave them the starting note with her recorder and they launched into the carol with enthusiasm. After they had finished, Pippa barked instead of applauding and they all looked expectantly towards the door in the hope that it would open. As it didn't, Emma knocked firmly on the door, but it still didn't open.

'Oh dear, perhaps they aren't at home after all,' said Katie in disappointment.

As they waited, they saw a Range Rover returning to the drive of the huge house next door.

'All right, let's go next door,' said Emma. 'We know those people are definitely in because we saw them drive home just now.'

'What shall we try this time?' asked Laurie. 'Shall we sing 'Away in a Manger' because everyone knows that one?'

Once again, they sang their hearts out, but the front door remained firmly closed. They waited for a while and then Emma knocked sharply on the front door.

'This is ridiculous. It's so rude when they know we know they're in!' exclaimed Emma. 'Last year, Miss Prendergast took the Grove Park school choir out carol singing around Broomstick Lane and the people came out in droves.'

'It seems they'll donate to the local grammar school, but not to anyone else,' said Lizzy drily.

'So, basically they're hypocrites as well as incredibly mean,' said Laurie, her lip curling with distaste.

'I suggest we give them a carol especially adapted to reflect their personalities!' proposed Emma and they sang very loudly:

> *'We wish you a stingy Christmas,*
> *We wish you a stingy Christmas,*
> *We wish you a stingy Christmas,*
> *And a Scrooge-like New Year!'*

They then slammed the letterbox hard and ran up the road giggling.

'Oh, I'm sorry everyone,' said Emma. 'We've wasted an evening and not collected a penny. Another stupid idea of mine, I guess.'

'Actually, doesn't the delightful Colonel Bolt-through-the-neck Granger live in Broomstick Lane?'

said Laurie. 'I think that might be his house down there.'

'Well, at least if we give up singing now, we'll be spared his pompous windbaggery!' said Lizzy and they laughed.

'As we're here, let's just have a quick look at his house,' said Emma. 'I'm interested to see it. Knowing him, it'll have stone lions and eagles outside and all manner of pretentious nonsense!'

They walked down the lane and Laurie said, 'I think this is the one'. As expected, the house was big but ugly with a Latin motto over the front door: *Carpe Diem!*

'What does "*Carpe Diem*" mean?' asked Katie.

'It means "Seize the Day",' explained Emma. 'I only know because my mum's a Latin teacher.'

As they walked up to the front door, Lizzy said, 'Has Colonel Granger got a family or does he rattle around this huge house by himself?'

'My dad told me his children are grown up now and his wife left him,' said Laurie.

'Can't say I blame her,' said Lizzy.

'Ssh,' said Katie in a hushed whisper. 'He must be home because his gold Jaguar's here. It'll be awful, if he should suddenly open the front door and hear us.'

'Oh, we can always burst into song,' said Laurie. 'After all, we genuinely are carol singing.'

'Albeit without any success so far,' added Lizzy drily.

'I must say it's rather a creepy house, in a funny sort of way,' said Emma, looking at the forbidding, dark façade surrounded by huge trees.

'Can't we just go home?' asked Katie uneasily.

At that moment, they could hear the front door being opened and they dived behind the large trees to the side of the house. Colonel Granger came out, leaving his front door open. He was carrying a large box, and quickly walked down the drive to his car. At that moment, Pippa unexpectedly tugged at her lead, taking Emma completely by surprise. Emma let go and, much to everyone's consternation, Pippa disappeared inside the house.

'Pippa, what're you doing?' whispered Emma, in anguish. 'Come back here at once.' There was no reply and no sign of Pippa. They looked at each other in dismay and then Emma also made a dash for the front door.

'Emma, don't go inside too!' said Lizzy.

'What on earth shall we do now?' said Katie, looking close to tears.

'I guess we'll just have to wait for Emma and Pippa to come out,' said Laurie.

'I fervently hope that's sooner rather than later,' whispered Lizzy.

'Oh, my goodness,' whispered Katie desperately.

'Here he comes. This seems like a really bad dream.'

As the Colonel walked back towards the house, lost in thought, Laurie swallowed hard and bravely emerged from the trees.

'Good evening, Colonel,' he said. 'I don't know if you remember me? I'm Laurie Price. You might know my mum as she's the district nurse for St David's.'

'Ah, yes, I do know her,' he said in surprise. 'Er, did you want something, Laurie?'

'Well, in a sense, yes,' said Laurie. 'You see, I'm carol singing in Broomstick Lane with my friends, Lizzy and Katie, and we really haven't had any success at all so far. You probably know them too, Lizzy Jones and Katie Edwards?'

At this point, Lizzy and Katie emerged sheepishly from the trees.

'Hello, Colonel,' said Lizzy. 'Katie was just helping me look for my glove.'

'We were just wondering whether we could sing a carol for you?' said Laurie rather desperately.

'We are collecting for charity,' added Katie. 'The church roof fund – such a good cause. You probably know that all of it was stolen from the church.'

'Yes, absolutely shocking,' he said. 'Well, I really don't have time for this but, since it is a good cause...'

'Oh thank you,' gushed Lizzy. 'Why don't you choose your favourite carol?'

'Very well,' he said, sighing in resignation. 'Let's have "Deck the Halls", but make it quick!'

The three girls began singing as loudly and merrily as they could under the circumstances. They only had the words for three verses so, when they got to the end, Laurie heroically burst into yet another round of 'Fa-la-la-la-la-la-la-la-la' with the other two following her lead.

'That's quite enough of that,' interrupted Colonel Granger. 'Here's two pence and good evening to you!'

The three girls looked up at him in dismay, but not one of them could think of any way to postpone the moment when he would re-enter his house. They watched him go in and shut the door firmly.

'Emma and Pippa are still in the house,' said Laurie mournfully. 'What on earth shall we do now?'

'I haven't given up hope that they'll find a way to sneak out without Colonel Self-Important noticing,' said Lizzy. 'Let's stay here to see what happens.'

While Emma's friends were trying to distract Colonel Granger, Emma was desperately hunting for Pippa inside the house.

'Pippa,' whispered Emma urgently. 'Where are you and what're you doing? I've never known you to be so naughty!'

The kitchen was in front of her so she tiptoed in, soon realising that Pippa wasn't there. After that, she went into the large living room next to the kitchen, where she found Pippa scratching at the door of a big wooden cupboard. She gave an excited bark when she saw Emma who rushed over to her and whispered, 'Pippa, there you are. Please be absolutely quiet and don't bark like that.' As Pippa continued to scratch at the cupboard door, Emma said in irritation, 'Have you gone mad, Pippa? You're going to get me into such trouble.' She opened the cupboard door in the hope that Pippa would stop scratching at it and, when she did so, beheld a china, turquoise, hexagonal teapot next to a shotgun. At first, her mind went totally blank with amazement, and then a number of thoughts and memories hurtled through her mind at once: Colonel Granger arriving at bell-ringing practice with a huge holdall; then staying downstairs to wash his hands before joining the other bell-ringers in the ringing chamber; the Colonel with his ostentation, huge house and gold Jaguar. Colonel Granger was the criminal, but much to her horror, she and Pippa were inside his house and he was just outside in the drive.

After a few moments, during which she felt powerless to do anything, Emma suddenly realised that, if she was going to act, she needed to do so quickly. She racked her brains and then remembered the camera in her bag. With her heart beating loudly, she got it out and, as quickly as she could, took several photos of the teapot, the cupboard itself as well as the living room.

'Thank goodness, this is a new film. Please, please, let nothing go wrong with my camera,' said Emma, as she picked up Pippa.

Just at that moment, she heard the living room door open and the Colonel came into the room. Emma's palms were sweaty and her heart was, by now, banging so loudly that she thought he must hear it. A look of amazement, which quickly turned to anger, appeared on his red face, and his grey moustache twitched.

'Emma Thomas, isn't it?' he said sternly. 'What on earth are you doing in my living room? I would not like to report you to your grandparents, or to the police, so I hope you have a good excuse.'

'I'm so sorry, Colonel,' said Emma. 'I was just outside and Pippa took it into her head to run into your house, so I just came in to find her. I really am very sorry. I have never known Pippa to be so naughty. I can't think what came over her,' she added, moving towards the door.

'Ah, were you carol singing with your friends outside?' he said, looking relieved.

'Oh yes,' said Emma. 'We've been carol singing up and down Broomstick Lane, but I can't say we've had any luck. Either people are out or don't seem to appreciate Christmas carols. We're collecting for the church roof, you know. Such a worthwhile cause.'

'Well, many of the people in Broomstick Lane are pillars of the community, you know, and don't have any time to waste on Christmas carols, even if they aren't quite as busy as I am. So, perhaps you and Pippa would now like to join your friends,' he said firmly. Emma saw his eyes turn towards the cupboard, with the turquoise teapot inside, and she started to feel faint.

'Certainly, and please do accept my apologies once more,' said Emma, edging out of the living room door just as fast as she could. 'Goodnight, and merry Christmas to you,' she added gaily.

Emma breathed a huge sigh of relief as she stepped into the driveway, still holding Pippa in her arms.

'Thank heavens,' said Laurie in relief.

'Are we glad to see you,' whispered Katie.

'Quick,' said Emma putting Pippa down. 'Let's get away from here as soon as possible and I'll explain everything.'

The others took her cue and ran down Broomstick Lane, along St David's High Street, past the Splash and towards Mabel's field by the church.

'Wait,' said Katie, pushing her fair hair out of her

eyes. 'I'm totally out of breath. Can't we stop running now?'

'Probably, we're far enough away and safe now,' said Emma, trying to catch her breath.

'What on earth is it?' asked Lizzy. 'Did that awful house turn out to be Bluebeard's Castle?'

'I really don't want to say anything until we get back to The Syngret,' said Emma.

They walked quickly down Church Lane to The Syngret where Emma directed them to the caravan. They all squeezed onto the seats around the small table.

'So, I know that was a bit scary,' said Laurie. 'We thought he was going to be furious to find you and Pippa in his house. But why're you being so mysterious?'

'You're not going to believe this, but Colonel Granger stole Reverend Pritchard's teapot,' said Emma.

'Haha,' said Laurie. 'That's a good one.'

'You're really serious, aren't you?' said Katie in wonder.

'What leads you to that conclusion?' asked Lizzy curiously.

'Oh, my goodness, if you don't believe me, what hope is there the grown-ups will?' groaned Emma, putting her head on the table.

'Well, none of us can stand him, so I'm sure we'd

be delighted to find he's St David's arch criminal!' said Lizzy.

'Come on, Emma,' said Laurie. 'Spill the beans.'

'Well, when I chased Pippa into the house, I found her scratching at a cupboard in the living room,' explained Emma. 'By chance really, I opened the cupboard door and there it was... the turquoise hexagonal teapot right next to a shotgun! And then it all made sense. I was there for the bell-ringing that evening when Reverend Pritchard discovered the teapot had been stolen. Who arrived late carrying a huge holdall and who stayed downstairs on his own to wash his hands before joining the others in the ringing chamber? Why Colonel Granger, of course. You gave us a clue, Laurie, but we didn't see it at the time.'

'Really? Did I?' said Laurie in amazement.

'Yes, don't you remember?' said Emma. 'At our Hallowe'en party we said that the Colonel must be rich because of his gold Jaguar. But, Laurie, you said people sometimes borrow money to show off before going bankrupt.'

'He must've been short of money and seized his opportunity,' guessed Lizzy.

'Yes, no wonder "Seize the day" is the motto above his door!' said Emma.

'Perhaps it should say "Seize the teapot" instead,' said Lizzy.

'How stupid of him to keep the teapot,' said Katie.

'I guess he didn't think anyone would look in his cupboard,' said Emma.

'He's also so arrogant he probably thinks no one would ever suspect him,' said Lizzy.

'And why does he keep a shotgun in his cupboard?' said Katie.

'Yes, that's really sinister,' said Lizzy.

'So, what do we do now?' asked Laurie. 'We don't have any proof.'

'Oh, yes we do,' said Emma. 'At least I hope we do. I took photos of the teapot in the cupboard and of the living room for good measure. Thank goodness I had my camera with me.'

'Well done, Emma,' exclaimed Laurie, her face lighting up. 'That really was great thinking on your part.'

'You clever thing!' said Katie in admiration.

'A total fluke really,' said Emma modestly. 'The question is: what do we do now? Do I have the photos printed and then take them to our grandparents or the police? Or should we tell them now?'

'It's a tricky one,' mused Lizzy. 'On the whole, I think we should tell them now. Then the police can get the photos produced at the police lab at top speed.'

'Yes,' said Laurie, 'and wouldn't it be terrible if

you took them to the chemist and they ruined, or lost, the photos?'

'Okay,' said Emma, taking a deep breath. 'Well, there's no time like the present, so let's go and tell them now.'

The others nodded solemnly and Pippa barked her approval.

Emma's grandparents were sitting in the living room.

'Granny, Gramps,' announced Emma. 'We've something really important to tell you.'

'Did anything happen when you were out carol singing?' said Granny in alarm.

'Yes, it did, actually,' said Emma, looking at Pippa. She and her friends explained what had happened and how Emma had come to find the large turquoise, hexagonal teapot.

'But are you absolutely sure, Emma?' said Grandpa in consternation. 'I know that no one can stand the man but he was an army colonel and is a Conservative Councillor. It'd be serious to accuse anyone of the theft, but especially him.'

'I can hardly believe it,' said Granny, looking upset.

'We thought it'd be best to tell Constable Roberts now,' said Emma. 'Then he can get the photos printed.'

'Emma, do you solemnly swear that you really

saw the teapot in Colonel Granger's cupboard?' said Grandpa earnestly. 'If this is a joke to teach him a lesson, it wouldn't be funny.'

'Yes, Gramps. I'm absolutely certain,' said Emma in earnest.

'Then, you and I will go to see Constable Roberts first thing tomorrow morning with the camera,' said Grandpa.

Emma's friends wished her good luck and goodnight.

'If Gramps and I can get to the police station early tomorrow, I'll still meet you at Mabel at 11.30am as usual. If I'm not there, you'll know I'm still at the police station,' said Emma.

The following day, Laurie, Lizzy and Katie arrived at Mabel promptly. They waited anxiously and were about to give up when Emma finally appeared, red curls flying as she raced towards Mabel, accompanied by Pippa sprinting at her side. She smiled and waved when she saw her friends in Mabel's branches.

'How did it go at the police station?' said Laurie.

'Phew, let me just catch my breath,' said Emma, climbing rather clumsily onto one of Mabel's lower branches. 'To be honest, Constable Roberts looked very dubious about the whole thing, especially as I had only recently told him the thief was Philip

Evans! But he did finally agree to get the photos printed as quickly as he could. Thank goodness Gramps was with me or I don't think he'd have done anything.'

'How terrible,' said Lizzy. 'So, presumably you can get away with murder if you're a pompous so-called "pillar of the community".'

'Let's not despair just yet,' said Katie. 'It doesn't mean he won't take any action when he has the actual evidence.'

'Unfortunately...' began Emma, 'Constable Roberts did point out that Colonel Granger could claim he has a teapot that looks exactly like Reverend Pritchard's.'

'What nonsense,' said Laurie in disgust. 'How many huge turquoise, hexagonal teapots are there in the world?'

'Constable Roberts is going to show the photos to Reverend Pritchard to see whether he can identify the teapot as his own,' said Emma.

'Well, you and your Grandpa have done everything you can,' said Katie, 'and I guess it's now in the lap of the gods.'

'Or the lap of Constable Roberts!' corrected Lizzy.

They jumped down from Mabel in a sombre mood and went home.

Chapter Twelve

Christmas Is Coming

As agreed, the following Saturday morning, Emma and friends met up in the living room of The Syngret. Emma had told everyone that Grandpa wanted to explain to them what had happened. They all arrived on time and sat down while Granny made everyone tea, with Edward's help, and brought in a Victoria sponge cake. Then, Grandpa joined them in the living room, accompanied by Constable Roberts.

'Good morning, girls,' Constable Roberts said, taking off his helmet.

They all looked surprised as they returned his greeting.

'Well, do sit down, Constable Roberts, and help yourself to cake,' said Granny.

'Girls, Constable Roberts was so impressed by your detective work that he wanted to come and tell you everything in person,' said Grandpa.

'We can't wait to hear what's happened,' said Katie.

'We've been hoping Colonel Granger would get his comeuppance,' said Lizzy.

'First of all, I had Emma's photos printed as a matter of urgency. Thank goodness, Emma had taken good shots, and the turquoise teapot was clearly shown in the cupboard in Colonel Granger's living room.'

Emma blushed at the praise.

'Yes, but we were worried he'd say he just happened to have a turquoise teapot exactly the same as the one in the church,' said Laurie.

'Ah yes,' said Constable Roberts. 'I took the photos to Reverend Pritchard who managed to identify the teapot as his. There were chips in the spout and lid and you can clearly see them in the photos.'

The girls clapped their hands in glee.

'After that, another police officer and I went to interview Colonel Granger in his house. We had a warrant to remove the teapot from his cupboard. As you can imagine, the Colonel was completely outraged and said he was going to contact his lawyer immediately. But then I mentioned that the Reverend Pritchard had identified that the teapot was definitely his, because of the broken bits.

Colonel Granger suddenly looked very shifty, bolted out of the front door, and drove off at top speed in his Jaguar.'

'Oh, goodness,' said Katie.

'We followed him in our patrol car and there was a high-speed chase through St David's. It looked as though we were about to lose him, but amazingly as he was approaching Fairdale Farm, Farmer Williams happened to drive his tractor out on to the lane. As you know, the road is single track there, so Colonel Granger had to slam on his brakes. He couldn't control the car and had to veer off into the field.'

'How exciting!' exclaimed Laurie.

'Luckily, no one was hurt, but the Jaguar wouldn't start again and Colonel Granger got out and started to run across the field. We followed hot on his heels. He ended up falling head-first into the duck pond at the end of the field, with the police having to fish him out. Unfortunately, his wig came off in the pond and we had to fish that out too!'

At this, everyone laughed and cheered.

'I'm afraid it really does serve him right,' said Granny. 'What a terrible thing to do.'

'When we finally got Colonel Granger to the station,' said Constable Roberts, 'I'm afraid he claimed he had never seen the teapot before in his life and that Emma must have planted it in his cupboard, when she and Pippa went into his house.'

Everyone looked shocked and Laurie declared:

'Are there no depths to which that man won't sink?'

'You didn't believe him, did you?' asked Emma tentatively.

'No, I didn't but what counts in a court of law is the hard evidence,' said Constable Roberts. 'When we got the fingerprint results back from the lab, yours weren't on the teapot. Of course, the charming Colonel could well claim that you were wearing gloves. However, there isn't any way he could account for the fact that both his and the Reverend Pritchard's fingerprints were on that teapot. That, as we say in the police force, clinches it. Colonel Granger will probably receive quite a long prison sentence because of the breach of trust involved.'

'Why do you think he did it?' asked Katie in wonder.

'It turns out he was very short of money because of his expensive tastes,' said Grandpa.

'Well, I can't say I have much sympathy for him,' said Granny. 'Most people round here are short of money and it doesn't make them criminals.'

'What about the shotgun?' said Lizzy.

'Colonel Granger did actually have a shotgun licence but, as you can imagine, he was supposed to keep the gun securely – not in an unlocked cupboard in his living room,' said Constable Roberts.

'I guess that's another law he broke,' said Granny.

'Girls, you did a marvellous job,' said Constable Roberts. 'Well done!'

Emma and friends all looked pleased.

'Do you know, I think the person we need to thank is Pippa,' said Emma. 'She was the one who ran into Colonel Granger's house and found the teapot in the first place.'

'Yes, that dog really is a genius!' exclaimed Lizzy.

'Three cheers for Pippa!' cried Laurie. They all cheered and Pippa barked in agreement.

The days were becoming shorter, darker and colder and everyone was starting to feel excited about Christmas, especially as Emma and Edward's parents were due to return from Cyprus for two weeks. Miss Prendergast had ambitious Christmas plans for the choir, so Emma's time was taken up with rehearsals. The music involved was beautiful and it was a real pleasure to learn.

The rehearsals culminated in the Grove Park school's carol concert, with the choir walking into the darkened assembly hall, and each girl carrying a candle-lit lantern, singing unaccompanied. By the time the whole choir reached their places on the stage, the sound was swelling into a resounding 'Alleluia'. Grandpa, Granny, Edward and Emma's three friends were in the audience, and Emma smiled at them when the lights came up.

The concert was very successful, with the school orchestra's brass section adding to the Christmassy atmosphere of the traditional carols. This included audience participation, as well as unaccompanied carols that showed off the choir's ability to sing very quietly to good effect. As the guest solo artiste, Farmer Williams sang 'Every Valley Shall Be Exalted' from *The Messiah*. The concert ended, once again in darkness, with the girls walking through the hall carrying their candles and singing:

> *Past three a clock,*
> *And a cold frosty morning,*
> *Past three a clock;*
> *Good morrow, masters all.*

When the lights came up, Miss Prendergast smiled and bowed and then held up her hands for quiet. 'Dear parents, friends and patrons, thank you for your appreciation. It means so much to me. It is a great pleasure to work with the choir of Grove Park and I'm delighted to have your thanks and support for my hard work and creativity. Thank you, once again.' She gave a royal wave as she walked through the hall smiling and nodding.

'Goodness,' said Granny. 'How unusual.

Conductors usually direct the audience's applause to the choir, orchestra and soloists, not taking all the praise for themselves.'

'I'm afraid that Miss Prendergast is a law unto herself,' whispered Lizzy.

'I think everyone knows my opinion of Miss Prendergast!' said Grandpa, raising his eyes to the ceiling.

They went into the school library, lit by golden candles and twinkling fairy lights, where mulled wine and mince pies were being served. They were joined by Emma and Richard.

'Congratulations to you both,' said Granny. 'Richard, you were as wonderful as always and, Emma, I think the choir was on its very best form.'

'Richard, when you were singing I felt as though I could actually see every valley,' said Grandpa.

'It was such a great concert,' said Laurie. 'It was lovely to hear both the unusual carols and the traditional ones where everyone could join in.'

'I liked the trumpets best,' said Edward. 'I hope, by next year, I'll be able to play in a carol concert.'

'With Mr Atkinson's help, I'm sure you will, my boy,' said Grandpa.

'Edith, darling, how lovely to see you.' They turned to see Cynthia crossing the library to greet them.

'Hello, Cynthia,' said Granny.

'Hello, Mrs Rogers,' said the children, with a marked lack of enthusiasm.

'Oh, goodness, I haven't seen you since Emma's birthday in the summer, have I?' cried Cynthia. 'Are you still performing your Spanish act?' She tittered in a very high-pitched voice.

'So, Cynthia, what brings you to the Grove Park carol concert?' said Grandpa.

'Ah well, my husband, Roger, is likely to become a councillor for St David's very soon. We're hoping he may be an MP one day, so we need to support local events, you know. And, of course, Audrey, or should I say, Miss Prendergast and I are very old friends. In fact, we were at school together. So talented, isn't she?'

'Yes, we were just saying the choir sang wonderfully well and, of course, Farmer Williams is an amazing singer,' said Granny.

'I must admit I prefer a baritone myself,' said Cynthia. 'Anyway, I must be off. A person in my position needs to mingle, mingle, mingle.' With that, she departed in a flurry of blue hair and false fur.

'Merry Christmas to you too, Cynthia,' muttered Grandpa.

'You have to hand it to Cynthia,' said Granny, chuckling. 'She does give us a good laugh!'

'I suppose there's absolutely no chance that she could have been in league with Colonel Granger?' said Emma and they giggled.

The following Saturday, Emma and friends met again at the usual time in Mabel's branches. They were wrapped up extremely warmly against the cold.

'What a pity our carol singing was such a disaster,' said Emma.

'I know,' said Katie miserably. 'What will happen to the church roof now?'

'Well, why don't we give it another try?' said Lizzy, sensibly.

'Yes, why not?' agreed Laurie. 'You know my mum's a district nurse and her area's Gresford, the council estate at the end of the village. She says they're a lovely bunch of people. Why don't we try there, this time?'

'What a good idea,' said Emma, perking up.

The following Friday, four girls and one poodle, decked out in their green and gold finery, walked through St David's streets, decked with strings of tiny golden lights, over to the Gresford estate. The doors were decorated with festive wreaths, and fairy lights twinkled in house windows and on many of the trees in the gardens. Here they received a warm reception with people requesting their favourite carols and often joining in, and the golden jam jar was soon full of coins.

A couple of hours later, four red-cheeked girls,

accompanied by one happy poodle, walked back home, delighted with their collection and the praise they had received, both for their singing and for their charitable intentions.

They soon reached Mabel whom they had decorated with a big, golden tinsel bow around her trunk! They wished each other, and Mabel, goodnight.

'Merry Christmas, Mabel dearest,' they said.

'See you at the Christmas Eve midnight service,' said Emma happily.

'Agreed,' said one and all, and Pippa pirouetted on the spot in celebration.

Granny and Grandpa always had a party on Christmas Eve for family members and neighbours. Gina, David, Sarah and Mark were due to arrive in the late morning in good time for the afternoon party. The plan was to attend midnight mass at St Mary Magdalene afterwards, and even Edward would be allowed to stay up for it.

Everyone spent the morning decorating the old house with coloured candles and twinkling lights, and the beautiful tree in the living-room proudly displayed the Christmas baubles and trinkets that Granny had accumulated over the years, which held many memories for the whole family. Grandpa ensured that Myfanwy was not forgotten, and the mermaid held a fairy wand and was dressed in a sequinned cape with a silver star on her head. By late morning, the wine was mulling and the glorious aroma of cinnamon, cloves and nutmeg wafted through the house and across the garden.

At around noon, a familiar red convertible drove into The Syngret's drive and the children jumped up and down in excitement. 'Auntie Gina, David, Merry Christmas!' cried the children.

'Woof,' barked Pippa.

'How lovely to see you,' called their grandparents.

Gina and David got out of the car, bringing into the house Gina's glamorous pink suitcases and lots of beautifully wrapped presents which were immediately placed under the tree in the living room. With everyone talking at once and Pippa barking gaily, it was difficult to hear what anyone was saying.

'How are you all?' exclaimed Gina. 'I must say that, apart from the general festive merriment, I'm really excited about seeing Sarah and Mark again.'

'Hear, hear,' said Grandpa. 'Do you know it will be a full year since we were together?'

'And, of course, it's longer for David and me,' said Gina, 'as last Christmas we were honeymooning in Elba!'

'Talking of Mum and Dad,' said Emma. 'Shouldn't

they be here by now?'

Granny looked at the old Napoleon clock on the mantelpiece (which had its own unique sense of time!) and said, 'Yes, I must admit I would have expected them to be here by now.'

At that moment, the owl hooted and Grandpa picked up the telephone. 'Sarah, dear, where are you? Ah yes, I see – what a nuisance. Well, it can't be helped. We're all looking forward immensely to seeing you, so let's hope there's no further delay with the trains.'

'What is it, Gramps?' asked Emma anxiously. 'Will they be able to get here today?'

'Yes, it should be fine,' said Grandpa. 'Wouldn't you know it, everything went well with the flight to Manchester, but there seems to be a signalling problem delaying trains from Manchester. They'll give us a ring as soon as they get to Llandudno.'

'I want Mum and Dad to be here now!' said Edward.

'So do we all, darling,' said Gina.

'Let's have a glass of mulled wine to lift our spirits,' said Granny. That's what they did and then everyone helped themselves to Grandpa's celebratory soup of happiness, French bread, and an assortment of cheese. Everybody chatted happily and much fun was had by all. As the afternoon wore on, neighbours started to arrive and Emma and

Edward were kept busy taking coats and handing round mulled wine.

The guests played charades in two teams, and once Farmer Richard had arrived, it was time to gather around the piano for his celebrated tenor medley from *The Messiah*. This was followed by everybody standing up to sing their favourite carols. Louis Armstrong's head was peeking out of Edward's pocket, and he was squeaking along to the carols. While taking a break for another glass of mulled wine, Richard said, 'Where're Sarah and Mark? Weren't they due to arrive by now?'

Grandpa shook his head. 'Unfortunately, Richard, there's some kind of signalling failure at Manchester and this has held them up. I asked Sarah to telephone me as soon as they reached Llandudno, but we haven't heard from them yet. Perhaps they decided to get a taxi from Llandudno instead and are en-route right now – let's hope so, anyway.'

At this, Emma slipped out of the room and up to her bedroom to shed a few tears. In particular, she had missed her mother so much. It seemed too cruel that, after a whole year, there was now yet another delay. Pippa came into the room and jumped up on the bed to nuzzle Emma. 'Thank goodness, you didn't get a job abroad,' said Emma, trying to smile and stroking Pippa's curly head. She suddenly became aware of another presence in the room and she looked up to see her mother standing in the doorway.

'Mummy, mummy, you came back to me,' cried Emma, rushing into her mum's arms. Mother and daughter clasped each other for what seemed like ages.

'Well, my darling girl!' said Sarah, through her tears. 'I'm here now.'

With that, Emma and her mum walked downstairs, arm in arm, back into the family party, and the very best of Christmases was had by all.

For Emma…

…and for Pippa

Acknowledgements

I would like to thank all my wonderful child supporters, who are:

Abigail Johnson
Adonis Polydorou
Afeefah Batool Usman
Alex Dodsworth
Alex Mitchell
Alexander Leatham
Alexandros Menidiatis
Alexandros Nicolaides
Alexandros Sergiou
Alexie Clutterbuck
Alfie Boyles
Alfie Gould
Alice Ayers
Alice Powley
Amelia Church
Amelie Barber
Amelie Lowe
Amy Emilia Wiethoff
Andreas Ioannou
Andreas Loizou
Angela Joy Baroro
Annabel Wiethoff
Annie Theyer
Arthur Ayers

Arthur Smith
Asher Runciman
Athena Menidiatis
Audrey Wills
Ava Clare
Azeezah Bano Usman
Beatrice Anne Samson
Beau Cleverton
Ben Collins
Blanca Haase
Bridget Anne Samson
Brodie McConnell-Titley
Caleb Hussein
Cara Littlewood
Cara Murray
Casey Titley
Catherine Waveney Alice Beales
Charalambos Ioannou
Charlotte Hunter
Christopher Edwards
Cormac Stephenson
Daisy Dellar
Daphne Faber
Darcey Hurley

Delyth Keil
Deniz Akalin
Dylan Daines
Dylan Fitzpatrick
Dylan Lambie
Dylan Savage
Dylan Walsh
Eddie Curtis
Eden Aziz
Edie Bower
Edward Spencer
Eli Wilson
Elias Grove
Elijah Foster
Elle Pink
Ellen O'Donnell
Elliott James Rennie
Emilia Garzennec
Emma Fielden
Erin Leatham
Eryfili Makriyiannis
Esme Brunker
Evagoras Nicolaides
Evie Mycock

Findlay Ward
Finlay Hutchings
Finn Henry
Fionn McGrath
Flynn Brown
Francesca Millfleet
Freddie Frith
Freddie Spencer
Gabriel George Säfstöm Wedgwood
George Nicolaides
Georgia Carlisle
Georgia Rose Thomas
Giacomo Piemontese
Harriet Hodson
Harry Colman
Harvey Bowie-Hill
Hector Grove
Henriette Helfman
Henry Williams
Hunter Brown
Isabel Jorge
Isabella Jones
Isabelle Robinson
Isobel Saward
Izabelle Hunter
Izzy Morgan
Jack Broom
Jack Doyle
Jacob Walker-Williams
Jackson Wheatley
Jake Littlewood
Jake Edwards
Jasper Cleverton
Jayden Klein
Jemima Newman
Jenson Clutterbuck
Jett Priestly
John Ioannou
Jonathan Wiethoff
Jordan Joseph
Joseph Hydes
Josie Colelman
Jude Bower
Kalomira Mae Gimutao
Kareena Doyle
Kiana Fayeye
Laney Moore

Leela Shivashankar Prickitt
Lenny Williams
Lewis Titley
Liliwen Joy Crafts-Rahn
Livvy Czyz
Lochlann Gaskin
Lola Robinson
Loukas James
Lucy Neaves
Lucy Spencer
Lucy Walsh
Luka Czyz
Luke Bowie-Hill
Luna Palumbo
Macie Moore
Macy Hibbett
Maggie Cockley
Maggie Harris
Maggie Prieto
Magnus Church
Manaal Christmas
Manos Kyriacou
Maria Lena Baroro
Maria Sotiria Markos
Marisa Peters
Marley Hibbett
Mary Harris
Matilda Gaskin
Matilda Smith
Matthew Dodsworth
Max Reddy
Mayia Loizou
Megan Dabell
Mia Pink
Micol Piemontese
Mila Piemontese
Mollie Helfman
Na'ilah Christmas
Nate Nicholls
Neophytos Ramos
Neve Fielden
Niall O'Donnell
Nicole Hadjievagorou
Oliver Williams
Olly McConnell
Oscar Gregory
Paddy George Mcnulty
Parker Czyz

Peggy Doyle
Peter Andreou
Piel Abby Tolentino
Pippa Cockley
Quinlan Foster
Rafael Papatheofilou
Reuben Gaskin
Riley Twinning
Riya Hird
Robyn Dabell
Romy Williams
Rory Salisbury
Rory Thomas
Ruby Simons
Sam Morgan
Samara Fayeye
Sara Hadjievagorou
Saul McGuigan-Seago
Scarlett Titley
Scarlett Wheatley
Scarlette Jillia Fabella
Shreya O'Donnell
Skye Lambie
Stella Simmonds
Stephanos Demetriou
Tayo Fayeye
Teigan Joseph
Themba Mashingaidze
Theo Newton
Toby Helfman
Toby Merhemitch
Thomas Cassie
Thomas Norman
Utku Akalin
Veronica Wheatley
Vinnie Mycock
Walter Coggins
William Spencer
William Theyer
Winston Grove
Yahya Usman
Zahrya Miller
Zander Neaves
Zoe Simmonds

Special thanks go to Sue Wheatley and the Bedford Girls' School Alumnae Association for recruiting so many!

I am particularly grateful to Edie Bower, my very first child supporter and reader – she encouraged me to continue investigating. I have also been very appreciative of my friend, Tamara Cizeika, for her boundless enthusiasm and support.

I would like to thank my friend, Jean Andrews, and my writing group for all their insightful comments: David Dyke, Barbara Kyei, Sarah Rosen-Webb, Debbie Singer, Pete Skyte, Roy Sunderland and Shula Wilson.